THE SPIRIT FLYER SERIES

THE LAST CHRISTMAS

The Holiday Scheme to Stop Spirit Flyers

JOHN BIBEE

Illustrated by Paul Turnbaugh

INTERVARSITY PRESS
DOWNERS GROVE, ILLINOIS 60515

© 1990 by John Bibee

InterVarsity Press is the book-publishing division of InterVarsity Christian Fellowship, a student movement active on campus at hundreds of universities, colleges and schools of nursing in the United States of America, and a member movement of the International Fellowship of Evangelical Students. For information about local and regional activities, write Public Relations Dept., InterVarsity Christian Fellowship, 6400 Schroeder Rd., P.O. Box 7895, Madison, WI 53707-7895.

Distributed in Canada through InterVarsity Press, 860 Denison St., Unit 3, Markham, Ontario L3R 4H1, Canada.

Cover illustration: Paul Turnbaugh

ISBN 0-8308-1204-0

Printed in the United States of America

Bibee, John.
     The last Christmas/by John Bibee.
       p.   cm.—(The Spirit Flyer series)
     Summary: With the ORDER party taking over the whole town of
Centerville, things seem so bad that Barry feels it will be his last
Christmas.
     ISBN 0-8308-1204-0
     [1. Fantasy]   I. Title.   II. Series: Bibee, John. Spirit Flyer
series.
   PZ7.B471464Las   1990
[Fic]—dc20   90-4870
                                                                              CIP
                                                                               AC

13   12   11   10   9   8   7   6   5   4   3   2   1
99   98   97   96   95   94   93   92   91   90

For the Oinklings

WHAT BARRY
FOUND AT THE
CLUBHOUSE
· · · · · · · · ·

1

Once there was a boy who waged a war
with fear. Deep inside, he felt that if he were just powerful enough or
brave enough, he could win and never be scared again. He struggled
with his fears, fighting them and fighting the others he blamed for
causing his fears. But when that battle crossed into the Deeper World,
he discovered that his fears had only begun . . .

Barry Smedlowe was afraid as he pedaled toward his clubhouse that
Thanksgiving afternoon. The sky was gray and cold. Brown leaves rattled
and blew across the dirty pavement. Barry zipped up his jacket as he
headed into the wind. A large dog, a black and tan Doberman pinscher,

ran steadily alongside the boy on his bike.

Even though he was afraid, Barry kept pedaling because he was on a mission of war. He was determined to protect his clubhouse from his worst enemy, Sloan Favor. The clubhouse was an old wooden shed in the alley behind the toy store. For almost a year, Barry and his friends had claimed the shed as their secret meeting place for the Cobra Club. The kids kept some supplies inside and Barry had put a lock on the door. But a few day before Thanksgiving, Barry had heard rumors that Sloan and his club, called the Super Wings, were planning to do something to the clubhouse. He wasn't sure if the rumors were true or not, but he planned to play it safe by putting a new, larger padlock on the clubhouse door.

Barry rode up Main Street. He frowned as he coasted to the intersection of Eighth Street and Main. The stoplight that led into the town square was blinking off and on in an erratic fashion. It was clearly out of order. Both the red and green lights would flash at the same time. Then the yellow would blink quickly on and off. Barry braked to a stop. The dog stopped too.

"Nothing works right anymore, Napoleon," Barry said with disgust as he stared at the sign. Even though the stoplight wasn't working, it didn't seem to matter. There was only one car moving, far down the deserted street. There wasn't a repairman or truck in sight. Barry spun a pedal of the expensive golden ten-speed bicycle which bore the name Goliath Super Wings. He looked down at the face of the large dog. He reached down to pat the sleek black and tan fur. The dog was only seven months old but already large for his age. His ears stood up in straight alert points. Barry patted his head. The streetlight overhead flashed on and off.

"Everything has been messed up since that crazy Halloween War," the boy grunted. He sighed, and then he pushed with one foot and began pedaling the sleek golden ten-speed bike down the street. Napoleon, his obedient dog, ran easily along beside the bike. The dog's toenails clicked on the pavement.

Barry was twelve years old and had straight black hair. He had a sturdy build and was tall for his age. Barry had an ordinary face, yet he frowned much of the time. He always looked on guard. His first reaction toward most people was immediate suspicion and distrust.

Since the Halloween War, as people called it, Barry was more suspicious than ever. Most people were cautious and for good reason. In those dark days following the war, the world had changed dramatically and was still changing. Everything had been very confusing for the boy. The whole country was under emergency martial law. Barry didn't understand it very well. He didn't know that it was possible for governments to go bankrupt and change so quickly. His father said it wasn't only due to the effects of the war and bombs on the coasts but also to economic conditions at home and in other countries around the world. He said it was like a big bubble of debt that had popped which in turn had broken the confidence of the people. Every nation had been drastically affected by what they called the Third Great Depression. Barry didn't understand his father's explanations about what had happened. All the boy felt was fear. He was afraid of all the sudden changes, afraid of what the future might bring.

Everyone seemed more afraid. That was why Napoleon was by Barry's side. After the war, there were reports of lootings and gangs roaming the streets, stealing from people and stores. Some gangs were said to be as big as small armies, but they were mostly in the cities and hadn't come to a small town like Centerville. But Mr. Smedlowe didn't want to take any chances. He had bought the big Doberman to protect the home and Barry. Barry was their only child and Mr. Smedlowe insisted that the big dog go with Barry if he went out of the house.

Barry was delighted to have Napoleon since he had always wanted a dog. At the same time, it reminded the boy how stubborn his father had been in not letting him have a dog sooner. Though Napoleon was actually quite friendly, as most Dobermans are, he looked scary, and that was what his father wanted—a big scary-looking dog that growled and barked loudly. The dog was loyal to Barry and the family. If he heard noises at night, he would bark and bark. Some nights the dog barked so loudly that Mr. Smedlowe often vowed he would get rid of him. But the dog stayed. Mr. Smedlowe felt that though he lost some sleep over the barking, he would lose more sleep if he didn't feel safe and peaceful.

The whole town had changed in a few days. The streets were strangely quiet and closed, like a ghost town. People stayed inside their houses much more of the time. Barry's dad had said Centerville was still in a state of shock even though it had been over four weeks since the war. There had only been a few bombs set off on the mainland and even they had fallen more than a thousand miles away from Centerville, yet the tiny town was still feeling the effects.

After the initial shock of the war, Barry had then felt irritated and bored for weeks. School had been canceled, not only in Centerville but in most places. Most kids were calling it the war vacation. Since the government had gone into such a shambles, everything had stopped. Offices had been closed, the electricity had been out, the phones had been out, and mail service had been cut. Even the toilets hadn't worked. Nothing had worked for the first few days. And since then, the government was still in confusion, limping along under military law. There were new rumors every day about what the future held. Some people said that the government had totally collapsed and worse problems were coming. Others claimed that the government was going to be all right. No one seemed to know for sure what was going to happen next.

Centerville, like so many other towns, was a town in waiting: waiting for order to come back so things would work again. Everyone wished things would return to the old days when the lights worked all the time, when you could cash a check at the supermarket and when gasoline didn't cost a fortune.

Barry wasn't thinking of any of those things that Thanksgiving Day.

All he could think of was Sloan Favor. Even with Napoleon at his side, Barry still felt uneasy as he pedaled down the alley behind the toy store. Barry and Sloan Favor had been enemies since the day Sloan had arrived in town in September. Sloan lived in a big house right across the street from Barry and both boys had immediately disliked each other.

Sloan was in seventh grade and very popular. He had blond hair, blue eyes, perfect teeth and practically everyone thought he was the most handsome boy in the school. He was good at sports and school work. He was full of self-confidence, and always assumed he was the best at what he did. Barry had invited Sloan to be a part of the Cobra Club the first day Sloan had arrived, but Sloan just laughed, acting as if he thought the idea was preposterous. Barry had been angry and thought Sloan was a royal snob.

Soon after Sloan arrived, most of the children in Centerville began competing against each other in a game called Caves and Cobras. Caves and Cobras, or C & C as most kids called it, was a role-playing war game where each person was on a team. The object of the game was to win the most treasure and "kill" the most enemies, which was anyone who wasn't on your team or in your club.

For most of the month of October, the kids had been waging war on each other out at a place everyone called Bicycle Hills. Barry was the leader of the Cobra Club's team. Sloan Favor was the leader of the Super Wings Club.

The games of Caves and Cobras had been a lot of fun at first, but somehow, it had turned into something more serious than just a game. It became difficult to tell the difference between what was pretend and what was real. Kids who had been friends before became more and more suspicious of each other if they weren't on the same team or club. They accused each other of being spies and stealers of secrets and game strategies. In playing the game, the children learned to deceive and betray one another until it was almost second nature to cheat or lie. The person who could be the most tricky often got the best score while playing the game because in a game of war, it was survival of the fittest and most cunning.

The final determining game of Caves and Cobras had been played on Halloween night. Barry's and Sloan's clubs had gotten the most points and the battle was really between them. But as it turned out, the war game ended and all the children were losers, trapped in the game cave. They had barely escaped.

Barry still had nightmares about that Halloween night. He wasn't sure if it was the war games or the real war with real bombs that kept giving him nightmares from that night. On that same Halloween evening, while children of Centerville were playing war, the real war in places far away from Centerville had started. The Halloween War, or World War Three, as many people called it, had been one of the shortest, yet most destructive wars in the history of the world.

Barry, like everyone else in the world, was still trying to adjust to the changes. One of the things that hadn't changed was the ongoing battle between Barry and Sloan. Barry was still fighting, still determined to gain victory over his enemy.

Since it was around lunchtime, Barry figured that Sloan and the other kids in his club would be at home eating. Barry had tried to get some of the other guys in the Cobra Club to help him put on the new lock, just in case there was trouble, but everyone had given him excuses. They claimed they were having special dinners or relatives visiting. Barry was disappointed and let his friends know it. He had openly expressed doubts about their loyalty. He had always been suspicious of his friends, but since the Halloween War, he was more suspicious than ever.

The alley was eerily quiet. Barry got off his bike and knocked down the kickstand. He walked carefully toward the clubhouse. Just as he reached into his coat pocket for the big padlock, he heard a shout. A mob of kids poured out of the wooden shed like a swarm of angry bees. Sloan was in the lead, an empty glass bottle in his hand. The other kids were holding bottles, rocks, and sticks of wood in raised arms.

Napoleon growled, but then yelped in pain when a rock thudded into his side. The big dog howled as another rock hit him, and then turned and ran down the alley.

"Come back, you stupid dog!" Barry yelled. A rock struck the boy on the leg. Barry dropped the lock and ran. He jumped on his bike just as a bottle sailed by his ear and exploded on the pavement in a loud pop. Barry stood up on the pedals of the golden ten-speed and shot down the alley. A rock bounced off his back in a thud. More rocks and bottles fell like rain around him as he sped away. He raced around the corner, followed by the jeers and shouts of the other boys. He sped onto Main Street. The boys were still after him.

Out of the corner of his eye, he saw one of the boys whirling something around his head. Barry pedaled faster. But it wasn't fast enough. He heard a whizzing sound, then a dreadful clatter on his bicycle. The back tire froze into a skid. A long Goliath Choker Chain, which resembled a dog chain, was wrapped up in the sprockets and around the frame of the bike so the wheel couldn't turn. The bike and boy rattled to a stop. Several spokes had snapped. Barry pulled at a loose end of the chain.

"Come on!" Barry muttered. He looked up. Sloan Favor was in the lead as the group of attackers charged down the street. Sloan was smiling, but his blue eyes looked deadly serious. The other boys' hands were holding rocks and bottles.

Barry stood up and let his bike fall to the street. Without looking back he began to run. He ran as far as the corner before looking back. He stopped. Sloan and the other boys had stopped by the fallen bicycle. They laughed and yelled at Barry, taunting him to come get his bike. Sloan then began to run toward Barry. Barry turned and ran. Sloan and the other boys hooted and jeered as they watched Barry escape.

Another person was watching Barry escape too. A man sat in a black jeep on a side street. The jeep had a single red light on the top that made it look official, like a police car. The sign on the side door said *ORDER*

17

Security Squad. The man inside wore a gray uniform with stripes on both shoulders and a patch over his heart which had a white circle with an X inside. He seemed to watch with great interest as Barry ran through the yard and down the street. He leaned forward. He kept staring until the boy disappeared around the corner. Then he reached down and started the engine.

Barry didn't slow down until he reached Buckingham, which was the street where he lived. He stopped and gasped for air. He jumped in fear when he heard a bicycle behind him. He began to run and then looked back. He was surprised and relieved to see that it was only John Kramar pedaling his old red bicycle, the Spirit Flyer.

"Didn't mean to scare you," John said pleasantly.

"Oh, shut up," Barry grunted. He was still breathing hard and looking suspiciously at the old red bike. Barry had been around Spirit Flyer bicycles before, but he never understood how they worked. To Barry, they were tricky bicycles, and he didn't trust them. Several months before, he had even tried to steal that same bicycle of John Kramar's and had had a nightmare of an experience. Barry had considered John and his strange old red bicycle enemies. Yet John was acting friendly on that Thanksgiving Day.

Just then, Napoleon, Barry's big Doberman pinscher, rounded the corner. He still looked afraid. And when he saw John Kramar, he looked mean. He bared his teeth and barked, heading straight for the boy on the big red bike.

"Tell him to stop," John yelled. He began pedaling the old bike. Barry was silent. The old bike sped up quickly. John headed down the street with Napoleon right behind him. Barry watched with angry satisfaction that someone else was being chased for a change. The bike was too fast for the dog. Barry frowned. Napoleon seemed useless. The boy muttered and then walked slowly toward his house. He didn't notice as the black jeep cruised slowly past the street behind him.

THE MAN
FROM ORDER

2

Barry was shaking as he walked up his front sidewalk. He felt so full of fear and rage that his stomach hurt. As he remembered his fallen bicycle and the way he ran, he also felt shame. Sloan had won again, and this time, the older boy not only had the clubhouse but also Barry's bicycle. Barry clenched his hands in fists and felt tears come into his eyes. He quickly wiped his eyes, looking both ways down the street, afraid that someone had seen him. All he saw was Napoleon. He yelled out to the dog. The big Doberman came bounding down the street.

"You worthless mutt," Barry snapped when the dog came running up.

Barry kicked the big Doberman in the side. Napoleon yelped and jumped away. Barry opened the front door and the dog ran inside.

Barry went in, slamming the door shut. Neither his mother nor father seemed to notice. Barry often slammed doors. He could hear his mother working in the kitchen, and he figured his father was in his office behind the closed door.

Barry trudged upstairs. He was about to go into his room when he stopped. Across the hall was an open door. The door was usually closed. He walked over and looked carefully inside. He paused, then walked into the room.

The room always seemed too quiet to the boy. There was a bed with a neat bedspread, and a chest of drawers with a photo album lying on top. The closet was open, but it was empty except for three bare wire hangers on a wooden rod. No one lived in the room. No one but a ghost, Barry thought. The room had once belonged to Barry's older brother, Bobby. But Bobby had died four years ago that summer. He had been at a summer camp and had drowned in a river. He had been a good swimmer. No one knew why he had drowned. It had just happened.

Barry hardly ever went into Bobby's old room. The place gave him the creeps and made him remember too many sad things. Even his parents hardly ever went into the room. His grandmother would sleep there if she came to visit, but it didn't seem to bother her. She still talked fondly about Bobby around the dinner table. Everyone had liked Bobby. He had been very popular in his class. He had been good at schoolwork and was exceptional at sports, especially at baseball. He had been twelve years old when he had died.

"The same age as I am now," Barry thought to himself. Though Bobby was gone, they all still lived with him. He was the unmentioned one. His parents seldom talked about Bobby, but Barry could tell they still thought about him. Both his parents had changed after his death. With Barry as their only child, Barry sometimes felt suffocated by their attention and expectations. It was as if he had to take the place of Bobby and be himself too. Barry knew he never measured up to Bobby's perform-ance in school or in sports, but deep inside he felt as if he was always expected to try.

Living with a ghost wasn't easy. The first year after Bobby died, Barry did so poorly at school that he had to repeat second grade. The pressure just wouldn't go away. The more his parents seemed to want Barry to replace Bobby, the more confused and angry Barry felt over the years. Though they had been great friends, Barry soon began to resent Bobby for dying.

Somewhere along the line, Barry gave up trying to be like Bobby. Instead, he began acting tough and mean. In his class, Barry began to be known as a bully. But his mother and dad hardly seemed to notice. They still wanted to see Bobby. They pretended Barry wasn't as bad as the teachers and other parents said. They made excuses and spoiled Barry. Since Mr. Smedlowe was the school principal, he used his influ-ence at school to keep Barry out of trouble. Barry was seldom punished for doing something wrong at home or at school.

His mother did everything she could to make Barry popular with the other children. When Barry had started the Cobra Club, Mrs. Smedlowe made sure they had plenty of good food, drinks and candy when the other boys came to the Smedlowes' house. All the kids liked to go swimming, so they had an open invitation to use the Smedlowes' pool. Though Barry was glad the kids in the Cobra Club came over, he secretly wondered if they would still come over if the sodas and candy stopped.

"They liked me for who I am," Barry whispered to himself. "I was Number One on the Point System, wasn't I? And I was always in the top twenty even after that creep Sloan stole my place. Things are just mixed up now because of that stupid Halloween War!"

Barry looked down at the photo album. He opened it. There were lots of pictures. Bobby on the pitcher's mound. Bobby at bat. Bobby sliding into home plate. He turned the page. There were more pictures of Bobby playing baseball. There was one photograph of Bobby sitting on a big red bicycle. Barry was about to turn the page when he felt something strange. He looked back at the picture of Bobby on the bike. Somehow the bike looked very familiar. The tires were big balloon tires. There was an old headlight and a horn. Barry squinted. The bike looked like . . . like that crazy bike of John Kramar's, the Spirit Flyer brand. Barry looked closer to see if he could make out the name. He was sure it was the same kind of big ugly bike. He could almost read the white letters . . .

Just then he heard a clatter. Outside, some kids hooted and hollered. Barry ran across the hall into his room. He looked out the window. A mangled golden bicycle was on the front lawn.

"My bike," Barry moaned. Across the street he saw the garage door closing on the Favor's house. He saw several legs just before the big door shut.

Barry rushed down the stairs and ran outside. He stopped when he got ten feet away from his bike. It was a mess. The tires had been slashed with knives. The front wheel was bent and most of the spokes were broken or bent as if someone had stomped on it. And the chain was off the sprockets, cut neatly in two with bolt cutters. Even the sleek frame was dented and smashed from blows by a sledgehammer.

A note was taped to the handlebars. He picked up the piece of paper. "Keep Centerville clean. Keep your garbage off the streets!" The words were written in thick red ink.

Across the street, the big garage door on the Favor house opened a crack. Barry picked up the bicycle and dragged it toward his own house. He heard laughter coming from across the street. Barry felt the rage and shame boiling inside. He wanted to whirl around and charge the other boys, but he knew he didn't have a chance.

He pulled the bike through a wooden gate around to the back of his house. He closed the gate and leaned his bike against the two metal garbage cans. The once beautiful golden bike did seem ready for the trash man.

Before Barry could decide what to do about his bicycle, he heard another noise out in the street. He opened the gate to peek out. A black jeep with a red emergency light on top was stopped in front of Barry's house. A white circle with an X inside was painted on the side of the door. A man in a gray military uniform was walking up the sidewalk.

Barry ran around to the back door. His mother was in the living room. The door to his father's office closed just as Barry ran up to his mother.

"Who was that?" Barry asked.

"That's Captain Sharp from the ORDER Security Squad," Mrs. Smedlowe said. "He's here to see your father about the school situation. School may be starting a week from next Monday, we hope."

"Oh," Barry said. His mother went back into the kitchen. Barry listened to the voices behind the closed door but couldn't make out what they were saying. He was curious. He had seen Captain Sharp before. His black jeep had been parked in front of the Favor's house several times. Mr. Favor was an important man out at the Goliath Factory and in the ORDER political party.

"But my dad is an important man too because he's the principal," Barry thought to himself. Barry walked slowly back upstairs. He looked down at the black jeep. Before the war, Barry had seen news reports on television about how the ORDER Security Squads worked in other cities and towns helping the local police and law enforcement agencies. The ORDER political party and Goliath Industries had created the Security Squads to help protect their many factories and businesses all over the world. Over a few short years, they had become the largest private police force in the world. Some people said they were like Goliath Industries' private army. The ORDER Security Squads were known to be tough and effective.

Ever since the war, the black ORDER Security Squad vehicles had become common in Centerville. Goliath Industries paid for the Security Squads not only to keep watch out at the Goliath factory but to help out all around the town. Most people were glad that the Security Squads patrolled the town as added protection.

A week after the war, Goliath Industries had quickly built a big new compound out on Cemetery Road on the land that had once been called Bicycle Hills. The Goliath employees had worked around the clock on the project. Everyone in town had been surprised how fast it had been built. The Security Squad Center, as it was called, was surrounded by a tall cement block wall with barbed wire at the top. A large, four-story cement-block building stood behind the walls. A lot of the Security Squad people lived at the center. They also kept their jeeps and trucks inside the walls at night. Barry had ridden by the place a number of times. The gray walls and the big gray block building inside reminded Barry of a prison.

The ORDER political party seemed to be involved in everything in Centerville. Barry wasn't surprised to hear that they wanted to help the school. He wondered if school would really start again. He hoped so. Barry flopped down on his bed. He wished things would go back to the way they were before the war. He missed the routine of school, of seeing his friends and the other kids in his class on a regular basis. Barry was still daydreaming about the way things had been before the war when he heard his father's office door open.

Barry hopped up and ran down the stairs. Mr. Smedlowe was smiling as he came out of his office. Captain Sharp smiled at Barry. He was a tall man, with a square jaw and short black hair. He stood very straight. His gray uniform was clean and crisp. His black boots were shiny.

"This must be Barry," Captain Sharp said. The man in the gray uniform snapped his heels together and then folded his arms across his chest like an X, both hands making fists. "Peace and safety," Captain Sharp said crisply. "That's the motto of ORDER."

Then the man in the gray uniform shook Barry's hand. The Captain's large dry hand had a very strong grip. Everything about the Captain seemed important and official, and the boy liked it. Mrs. Smedlowe walked into the room.

"Will school be opening again?" Mrs. Smedlowe asked.

"In a word, yes," Captain Sharp said. He bowed slightly in Mrs. Smedlowe's direction. "I was just bringing your husband the good news. Thanks to ORDER working across the state, we've mobilized enough resources to start school for long enough to carry us through until the elections in December. And once we have a mandate, and the new government in order, we assume the school situation will be secure. We can't let the youth of our great land waste any more time."

"I'm glad to hear that," Mrs. Smedlowe said with a smile.

"Of course, there will be some changes and adjustments in the school system as time goes by," Captain Sharp said. He smiled at Mr. Smedlowe.

"You'll still be principal, won't you, dear?" Mrs. Smedlowe asked her husband.

"Of course," Captain Sharp said with a smile. "A man with Mr. Smedlowe's experience and loyalty is a valuable asset. He may even be in line for the position of superintendent one of these days."

"Captain Sharp says there might be changes in the school board and they might ask Mr. Horton to resign," Mr. Smedlowe said.

"Well, his term is practically over anyway," Captain Sharp said. "And he doesn't seem as progressive as we in ORDER had hoped. He's been dragging his feet on letting us put in the New Improved Big Boards at the school. We've heard rumors that he's actually been campaigning against the ORDER candidates in this next election. He's clearly a man without vision. We need people of action like your husband. He can see the future and do what needs to be done. We like that in a person."

"Will the Point System be operating again?" Barry asked hopefully.

"Of course," the Captain said. "We'll have New Improved Big Boards and a New Improved Point System, along with New Improved Number Cards to go with it."

"New Improved Number Cards?" Barry asked.

"That's right," Captain Sharp said. "These are a hundred times as good as the old cards. They are 'smart cards.' They have a new, revolutionary kind of computer chip inside that stores and collects more information faster and better than the old cards. But the new cards do more than keep scores. They'll hold a new identity number, a tax number and lots of other things. They are one of the essential tools that will get not only our country, but countries all over the world back in operating order so we can recover from this awful time of crisis. Before long, everyone in the world will have one. The whole Point System will be new and improved and better than ever."

"When will we get the New Improved Number Cards?" Barry asked eagerly. Ever since the war, the Big Boards and the Point System hadn't worked.

"The number cards will be distributed the day school starts, right?" Captain Sharp looked at Mr. Smedlowe.

"That's correct," Mr. Smedlowe said. He cleared his throat.

"We will have your full cooperation, of course?"

"You can count on me," Mr. Smedlowe said. He smiled, but Barry thought his father's smile looked forced. "ORDER also has some good ideas for ways our young people can get involved in the community by forming Commando Patrols."

"That's right," Captain Sharp said. "We in the ORDER party feel that our youngest citizens need to learn how to be better citizens and contribute to our society."

"You mean like what the Boy Scouts and Girl Scouts used to be?" Mrs. Smedlowe asked.

"That's correct," Captain Sharp said. "We want to mold young men and women. We want them to learn to think of others and not only themselves. They'll be involved in public service projects like picking up litter along the highways on weekends and fixing up the town park. Our young people need to know the value of a job well done."

"I like that idea, don't you, Barry?" Mr. Smedlowe asked with a smile.

"Sounds like a lot of work to me," Barry said slowly. He thought about all the litter and trash along Route 63.

"There'll be fun and games too," Captain Sharp said. "We in ORDER feel like it's best that there be a balance between work and play. We'll encourage both. Each of these new Commando Patrols will need leaders too. I've already heard good things about your abilities as a leader. I'm sure you'll have a large and powerful patrol under your command in no time. You would like to assume leadership of a patrol, wouldn't you?"

"Sure I would," Barry said, bursting out in a smile. Suddenly the new patrols didn't sound so bad. "I've already been president of a club, the Cobra Club, for almost a year."

"Barry's club has been very popular with the others," Mrs. Smedlowe said, beaming with pride.

"I bet I'll have the biggest club in town," Barry said quickly. "Will we have ranks and everything? I want to be a general."

"I'm glad to see you're so eager," Captain Sharp said with a smile. "I haven't seen anyone else so anxious since I talked to your neighbors across the street yesterday. That young Favor boy, Sloan, was ready to go out recruiting members for his patrol before school even starts up again."

"I think everyone is anxious for school to resume," Mr. Smedlowe said. "We appreciate all your hard work, Captain Sharp."

"Don't thank me. Thank ORDER," Captain Sharp said. "After all, I'm just doing my duty. I'll be talking to you later, Mr. Smedlowe."

Captain Sharp shook hands with each one. Then he stood up straight and crossed his chest with both arms. "Peace and safety," he said. Mr. Smedlowe nodded, and opened the door.

The Smedlowes watched Captain Sharp climb into his black jeep. He sped away without waving. Mr. Smedlowe smiled, and then closed and locked their front door.

BARRY CALLS
A MEETING
· · · · · · · ·

3

On Sunday morning, the day before
school was set to reopen, Barry Smedlowe woke up with a plan. For over
a week he had brooded about losing the clubhouse to Sloan and his
gang. He could still hear their jeers and laughs as they had chased him.
The story about how he ran away had spread throughout the town. He
knew Sloan and the Super Wings Club were still gloating and calling him
a chicken and all sorts of names. Barry boiled inside every time he
thought of them.

But the worst reaction had been his own club. The members of the
Cobra Club had been avoiding him, or so it seemed to Barry. Barry had

tried to get the others boys together for a meeting the day after Thanks-giving, but only one person showed up, Roger Darrow. So Barry called off the meeting.

Finally, on Saturday night, Barry called all the members of the Cobra Club again and invited them over for a meeting on Sunday morning. Barry told them he had a great plan to get the clubhouse back. Most of the kids in the club agreed to come.

Barry was nervous. When the phone rang, he jumped at the breakfast table. His mother answered it. She listened and seemed puzzled.

"Who is this?" his mother asked loudly into the phone. She waited. "I'm sorry, but it's hard to hear you. You'll have to speak up." Mrs. Smedlowe frowned as she listened. Mr. Smedlowe stood up from the breakfast table.

"I can barely hear you," Mrs. Smedlowe said loudly. "Hello? Hello? Can you hear, me, Josh?" Mrs. Smedlowe hung up the phone. She stared at her husband.

"Who was it?"

"Well, I think it was Josh, your brother's son," she said slowly. "But it was hard to hear. Maybe we should call them back. He sounded upset."

"Really?" Mr. Smedlowe asked. "Call back. I've been worried about them. I've only talked to him once since the war. They seemed to be all right then, even though they were near the border of the war zone."

Barry planned to listen in, curious about his cousin Josh, when the front doorbell rang. "I'll get it," Barry yelled. He ran to the door. He smiled when he saw fifteen members of the Cobra Club outside on the front lawn.

"Let's go into the garage," Barry said to the group. He ran down the front walk and opened the garage door. The other boys pushed their bikes inside.

"Where's your bike?" Jason asked as he leaned his Goliath Super Wings against the wall.

"Out back," Barry said quickly. "I suppose you heard how that rat Sloan ruined it."

Barry looked around the group defiantly, as if daring the other boys to speak. They seemed uncomfortable and unusually quiet.

"Why didn't you fight back?" a boy named Jason asked.

"There was nothing else I could do," Barry blurted out. "They came at me with rocks and bottles. You would have run too!"

"I was only asking," Jason said softly. "It's just that Sloan said, well, you know how he exaggerates . . ."

"Sloan Favor is a creep and a cheat," Barry said. "He ganged up on me, twenty or twenty-five against one. I hate his guts, and I'll get even with him if it's the last thing I ever do."

Barry began to curse and call Sloan and the Super Wings Club every bad name he knew. The more he talked, the louder he got. And as the names got louder and more evil, the members of the Cobra Club began to smile and giggle. They began to join in, calling Sloan and the others the worst names they could think of. Only when his father opened the garage door, did the name calling and cursing stop.

"We're just practicing on some club cheers, Daddy," Barry said quickly. "We'll be quieter."

When Mr. Smedlowe closed the door, the other boys laughed and smiled. Some patted Barry on the back. At last, Barry felt like his club was with him once more.

"We'll make Sloan Favor sorry he ever touched our clubhouse," Barry said defiantly.

"What do you want to do?" Roger Darrow asked. Roger hadn't been in the club very long and Barry wasn't quick to answer.

"I've got some ideas," Barry said. "But first things first. School will be opening. My mom said we can have a party tonight to celebrate. We haven't really had a chance to celebrate anything since the war. So tonight is the night. We can show some movies on the VCR and have ice cream and soda and all the junk food everyone can eat. She's inviting most of the kids in our class, and a bunch of other people too."

"All right!" Jason said. "I'm ready to party anytime." The other boys began to smile. They enjoyed parties given by the Smedlowes.

"We'll have a big party, and we'll all be in the top twenty when the Point System gets rolling again."

"You mean it's coming back?" Jimmy asked hopefully.

"You bet, and that's not all," Barry said. "Captain Sharp came to my house the other day and said there's going to be some new clubs in town once school starts. We can be a part of them. They're called Commando Patrols."

Barry began telling them all the things Captain Sharp had shared. Though most of the Cobra Club members had heard different rumors, they knew Barry was probably telling them the truth since his dad was the school principal.

"Tonight will be a great time to recruit new members into the Cobra Club," Barry said. "Then when we form Commando Patrols, we can all be together in the biggest and best patrol in town. We'll make Sloan green with envy."

"Sloan has been trying to recruit more kids for the Super Wings Club, I hear," Jason said slowly. "Since he's not sick anymore, he's been calling people up."

"So what?" Barry asked loudly. "We'll get the best ranks in the Point System, and everyone will be dying to get in our club."

The other kids were silent for a moment as they dreamed about the Point System and the Big Boards. No one was quite sure how the mysterious Big Boards worked. They were something like a computerized adding machine and scoreboard. Big Boards were made of a black shiny, plasticlike material in the shape of a rectangle. The smaller ones were usually seven or eight feet tall, about twenty feet wide and three inches thick. But they could be much bigger. The kids all wondered what the New and Improved Big Boards would be like.

The Point System was the reason the Big Boards existed. Everything about a person or group was broken down into points. The Big Boards kept track of these points for the Point System. Barry had not liked the Point System at first because it seemed like another kind of report card, only bigger. The Big Board not only kept track of all the students' grades and scores on tests, but it also kept track of almost everything you could imagine—from I.Q. points to grade points to good and bad points to overall personality and popularity points. Then those points, negative and positive, were all added up to form a person's overall point total or score. The higher your overall point total, the better your rank. And the better your rank, the more everyone thought of you.

Barry had started out in the coveted Number One position. He had felt like the king of the town. But then all that had changed. He had suddenly lost his rank. And he had never regained it. Once Sloan Favor had come to town, the popular new boy had been in the Number One position until the war when the Point System and Big Boards had stopped working. Barry had been anxious ever since, wondering where he ranked overall.

"I can hardly wait until tonight!" the president of the Cobra Club said. Then he raised his fist into the air. "We'll show Sloan who's Number One in this town." Barry smiled as the other boys clapped and cheered.

At six o'clock, children and their parents began arriving at the Smed-lowe's back-to-school party. The weather was unusually warm that evening for December. As principal, Mr. Smedlowe decided it would be a good idea to have a party for the adults as well. Mrs. Smedlowe had made several batches of super chocolate chip cookies. The table in the family room was filled with chips, pretzels, candy and dip. There were lots of little cut-up vegetables and pieces of fruit. The refrigerator was packed with cans of cold soda. There was also lemonade and tea and drinks for the adults. The ping-pong table was set up in the garage. Some kids were already playing in a tournament.

Barry opened a can of root beer and smiled. For the first time since he had lost the clubhouse, he began to feel better. The house was noisy with voices. Everyone looked like they were having a good time. Soon the street was filled with parked cars.

"Great party, Barry," Samantha Reeves said. Samantha was a seventh grader. Barry smiled and nodded. He went out to the garage to watch the ping-pong game. Roger and Alvin were playing against Jason and Scott.

"Aren't you going to call a meeting or something?" Scott asked. "The party's been going an hour."

"Yeah, after awhile," Barry said. He opened the garage door. Several people were standing on the lawn talking, sipping on their drinks and nibbling off plates of food. Barry stared across the street at the Favor house. Barry's mother had invited all the Favors to the party though Barry had protested loudly. Mr. Smedlowe said it was the only polite thing to do. Barry wasn't convinced. Fortunately, Sloan was nowhere to be seen. In fact, Barry hadn't seen any of the Super Wings club members either though his mother had invited several of them as well.

Down the street, Captain Sharp's black jeep turned the corner onto Buckingham. The red light was flashing on top as he slowly made his way past the parked cars. The black jeep turned into the driveway of the Favor house and stopped. As Captain Sharp got out, he turned off the flashing red light. He walked up the steps and the front door opened before he knocked. He went inside and the door closed. Barry stared at the Favor house enviously. He wondered why Captain Sharp had gone there.

Just then, a group of parents and children walking down the sidewalk crossed the street and walked over to the Favor house and knocked on the door. The door opened and they went in. Barry frowned as another family walked up to the front door of the Favor house. The kids playing ping-pong stopped.

"What's Captain Sharp doing over at the Favors' house?" Jason asked.

"Who cares?" Barry said. "He'll be over here in a minute. My dad invited him to our party."

A group of kids came down the street. They walked up to the Favor front door and went inside.

"That was Larry and a bunch of those Super Wings kids," Roger said. Then another family came down the street and crossed over to the Favor house and went inside.

"Why's everyone going over there?" Scott asked. "Are they having a meeting or something?"

The garage door of the Favor house rolled open slowly. Barry frowned when he saw Sloan and Tiffany Favor talking to Captain Sharp. Sloan and Tiffany followed the Captain to his black jeep. The man in the gray uniform opened the door. He seemed to be explaining something to the two children. Sloan reached inside by the steering wheel.

Suddenly the air was split with the sound of a siren. Everyone stopped talking. Sloan let it roar, whoop and wail for about fifteen seconds. Then he turned on the flashing red light on top of the jeep. The light blinked brightly like a beacon out into the street. Sloan walked back into the garage.

"What's he doing?" Jason asked.

Before anyone could answer, loud pulsing rock music filled the air. Barry squinted in surprise. The music was blaring out of two large speakers at the front of the garage. The red light on the jeep was still spinning and pulsing so it seemed almost driven by the music. Children began coming out of the Smedlowe house to see what was going on. Barry frowned as more kids came outside. Some were pointing at the Favor's house.

Captain Sharp walked briskly across the street. He smiled and nodded at the adults standing on the lawn. Then he went in the front door of the Smedlowe house.

"Now Captain Sharp is coming to our party," Barry said confidently.

"But what's Sloan doing?" Jason asked.

"Causing a nuisance," Barry replied. "We ought to call the cops on him for disturbing the peace. I think I'll make the call myself."

"You wouldn't do that, would you?" Scott asked.

To answer, Barry turned and walked through the garage and into the house. His father and Captain Sharp were smiling and talking. Barry didn't wait to interrupt.

"Dad, I think we're going to have to call the cops because Sloan Favor is making a real noise out in the street disturbing the peace," Barry said, trying to sound serious like an adult. "I guess I should make the call since I heard it first."

"Nonsense," Mr. Smedlowe said and laughed. "The Favors are having a party too. Captain Sharp was just telling us that we're all invited over. He wants to hold a short little meeting over there since the Favor's living room is bigger. Tell your friends they're invited too."

Before Barry could say a word, Mr. Smedlowe announced the meeting to the guests in the living room.

"All you kids are welcome too," Mr. Smedlowe said loudly. "I understand Sloan has some fun in mind for you."

Barry was speechless. Before he could utter a word, the other children began streaming out of his house across the street toward the pounding music and flashing red light. He ran outside. "Wait!" he yelled to the Cobra Club members, but they were already in the Favors' garage. Barry ran down to the edge of his lawn. "Come back. I'm calling a special meeting of the Cobra Club right now."

No one was listening. Barry stood on the edge of his front lawn, refusing to take another step toward the Favors' house. Across the street, in front of his garage, Sloan Favor stared at Barry. Then Sloan waved. Only he was waving good-by.

Barry turned and stomped back into his house. He stomped into the kitchen and sat down at the table. He was too angry to eat or drink or do anything. All he could think about was that Sloan Favor had stolen his whole party right before his eyes.

Barry sat in steamy silence for several minutes. The house was empty.

He stared at the stacks of chips and food on the table. Barry heard the front door slam. When he looked up, he saw Alvin.

"Hey, Barry, you should come over to the Favors' house," Alvin said. "Ol' Sloan really knows how to throw a party. He's got one of those new digital, wall-screen TV's with these great video games. Someone said he even has a bootleg version of that new Caves and Cobras video game. It hasn't even been released in stores yet. I guess his dad can get it because he works for Goliath. Kids are dancing, and you know what, Sloan has a ping-pong table, a pool table, a regular hockey game and an air-hockey game. You should see his room! I just came to borrow a ping-pong paddle. Well, I'll see you in a little while."

Barry didn't say a word. He looked at his hands. Alvin slowly backed out of the room. Barry looked out of a window. He could see the glow of the flashing red light and hear the distant music.

CAPTAIN SHARP'S ANNOUNCEMENT
· · · · · · · ·
4

The war vacation was finally over. On Monday morning, December eighth, the doors of the Centerville School officially opened for the first time since Halloween. Though only three of the big yellow school buses ran their old routes that morning, the children arrived, either walking or getting a ride from their parents. Because of the confusion, the school day started an hour later than normal.

Barry went to school with a bad attitude. He was embarrassed to be seen on his old blue single-speed bike. Barry was at the bicycle racks, locking his front tire with a chain, when over a dozen kids on big red

Spirit Flyer bikes coasted up. John Kramar was in the lead. John got off and looked at Barry. "What are you staring at?" Barry demanded. Before John could answer, Barry turned and strode off toward the school door.

By nine o'clock, Barry was back in his old home room. Mrs. Johnson was still his sixth-grade teacher. Barry took his old seat, as did the other children. Some seats were empty. At 9:05 a bell rang. Mrs. Johnson called the class to order. She welcomed them back and then called out the roll. Barry looked glumly around the room. John Kramar was still there. Amy Burke, a neighbor of Barry's, was in her old seat too. Since she rode a Spirit Flyer, Barry didn't like her. Tiffany Favor, Sloan's popular sister, was whispering excitedly to some other girls. At least five kids in the Cobra Club were in Barry's room.

Mrs. Johnson announced they were going to have a welcome-back assembly. The class walked more quietly than usual to the auditorium and took their seats. Mr. Smedlowe was on the stage. The curtains were closed. Captain Sharp was standing near the curtains, tall and alert, smiling at the children. Barry stared at the man in the gray uniform. He seemed so sure of himself, Barry thought.

When all the classes of children were seated and settled, Mr. Smedlowe stepped up to the microphone. "I'd like to welcome you all back to school," Mr. Smedlowe said.

The children nodded and a few clapped their hands. Then they all began clapping. Some whistled, some cheered. Barry found himself clapping as hard as everyone else. The mood wasn't quite like anything Barry had experienced before. The attitude of the children wasn't like coming back from summer vacation. Barry looked at the faces of the children near him. They were relieved to be back in school and grateful. School was what everyone was used to as a way a life. Barry could feel the same longings inside himself as he clapped even harder. When the clapping died down, Mr. Smedlowe leaned closer to the microphone.

"I'm glad you are all so eager to get on with your studies," Mr. Smedlowe said. "And I think I speak for all the teachers and staff when

I say that we're glad to have you back."

Most of the teachers clapped. The children whispered and smiled. Mr. Smedlowe clapped a few times and then cleared his throat. "Your teachers, of course, will help you get back into the routine of your studies," Mr. Smedlowe said. "But today, we have a special treat, one I think you'll all enjoy. Captain Sharp is here to visit with us. He is an employee of Goliath Industries in their Security Squad division and active in the ORDER political party. Goliath Industries and the ORDER party, as many of you may know, have helped get our school back on its feet. Let's all give Captain Sharp a warm welcome."

The children applauded again as Captain Sharp walked quickly to the microphone. He smiled. Then with a wave of his arm, the lights in the room dimmed. Loud music sounding like a cross between a rock song and a march filled the room.

Like everyone else, Barry was sitting forward in his seat to see what was behind the curtains. At first it appeared to be only darkness, but then, just as the music got the loudest, the darkness burst into a flash of light. Beams of laser light flashed over the crowd of children in time with the music. The lights split the darkness as the music pounded, louder and louder, until it reached a peak. As the cymbals crashed, horns screamed and the synthesizers wailed, the curtain covering the stage began to open and a long rectangular panel came into view. The panel appeared to be twenty feet tall and forty feet long, as big as the stage itself. Drums boomed like firing cannons as words lit up on the dark panel:

****

ORDER WELCOMES YOU
TO A NEW BEGINNING!

****

The children in the audience clapped and whispered. Then more words flashed up on the screen:

****

WELCOME TO THE NEW POINT SYSTEM!
WELCOME BACK TO SCHOOL!

****

"A new Big Board," Barry said softly. Only this was the largest Big Board he had ever seen. And somehow it was different than the old Big Boards. The words had brighter colors and were more three-dimensional.

Then the music erupted loudly as the long black panel began to flash again. Bolts of laser light shot into the air as fast as a firing machine gun. The Big Board lit up again, only this time, below the words, a huge image appeared, something like a television screen—only much larger, like a movie screen. Barry quickly realized it was one of the new kinds of digital television panel-screens. With the newer TV screens, the picture could be made any size, big or small, on a very flat panel. The images were sharp and clear.

The first image was an explosive shot of a bomb going off. A large mushroom cloud rose into a crisp blue sky. Barry felt an immediate shock pass through his body as he remembered the war. That single image united every child in the room in a fear that they had all shared. The next image was of buildings knocked down and streets filled with rubble.

Then there was a picture that made everyone look closer. At first Barry thought it was a person lying on her back. Then he thought it was a doll, and then he finally realized it was a statue. It was a moving picture taken from a helicopter. As the camera zoomed in closer, every school child recognized the Statue of Liberty lying on its back as if it were dead. The crown on the statue's head was partly crushed. The face stared blindly up at the sky. The image faded into darkness. The children in the crowd

murmured. Right after the war, pictures of the fallen statue had been on every TV screen and magazine and newspaper in the world. Barry thought he heard a sniffle.

The screen came to life again. This time it was a pretty field of flowers. Birds were singing. Bees were buzzing about. "This is a time for new beginnings," a voice said over the speaker. "Out of the rubble and ashes of conflict, we must rebuild for the future. And ORDER is leading the way to a new peace and safety in our land, in our world."

Barry stared at the big screen with an open mouth as more images flew by. There were bulldozers moving earth and carpenters hammering, cranes putting up steel girders on tall buildings. Each image was someone building something. The people working looked determined, yet happy. There were images of kids playing baseball and going to school.

The next image surprised Barry slightly. The kids at the school on the screen all wore gray uniforms like Captain Sharp's. They had the sign of the circled X over their hearts. They stood up in line. They all saluted, their hands across their chests, and looked right out at the audience of children. "Peace and safety," the children said in unison.

Then there was a picture of children holding small black cards about the size of credit cards. They were lining up to eat in a cafeteria, but before they picked up their trays, they would push the black card into a slot above the silverware bins.

Then there were more pictures of children buying things at the grocery store or the shoe store or the toy store. And each time they bought something, the children smiled and gave the checkout person their number card, which was placed into a slot in a small black box beneath a computer screen.

The screen then showed children playing soccer. They were happy and laughing. The uniforms were the same. Each one had a patch over the heart with the sign of the white circled X. The camera froze on the circled X.

"On with the future," the voice boomed. "Let's get our world in ORDER."

The screen was filled with smiling faces of men and women and children, looking upward, their hands crossed on their chests. "Peace and safety to all," they shouted. Then the music played. The lights came back on. The children began clapping as Captain Sharp walked across the stage. He snapped his heels together and folded his arms like an X across his chest.

"Peace and safety to each and every one of you," Captain Sharp said with a smile. The children clapped.

"Peace and safety to you," a boy shouted out. Then he stood up. It was Sloan Favor. He stood down near the front of the auditorium, his arms folded across his chest. At first Barry thought Sloan would get in trouble. But Captain Sharp smiled and nodded at Sloan. Then other boys next to Sloan stood up and crossed their chests with the ORDER salute, saying, "Peace and safety." When Captain Sharp smiled, kids everywhere leaped up, imitating the others, greeting the Captain. Barry stood to his feet, crossing his arms across his chest.

"Peace and safety to you," Barry yelled, hoping the Captain had heard him. Soon the auditorium was filled with standing children, their arms folded in salute. But not everyone was standing. Barry noticed that John Kramar and some of his friends were still sitting, whispering to each other. Barry frowned.

"You may be seated," Captain Sharp said. As the children sat down obediently, Captain Sharp walked across the stage and returned with a cardboard box. He set it by his feet. He bent down and pulled out a small black rectangle that looked like a credit card. The children began to whisper excitedly.

"As most of you have guessed," Captain Sharp said. "I'm holding one of the New Improved Number Cards."

The children whistled and clapped. Barry whistled as loud as he could.

"I don't guess I need to explain the Point System to such a bright group of students," Captain Sharp said with a smile. "But there are some changes in the new cards, so please listen carefully." The room became as quiet as a tomb. Captain Sharp smiled. "In a few minutes, you will be dismissed, and one by one, your classes will be going to the gymnasium where each of you will be assigned your New Improved Number Card," the captain said. "The Point System will work more or less the same as in the past. All your point totals will be kept track of by the Big Boards. Your school grades, test scores, your I.Q., and all those other areas of performance that make you the person you are will be broken down into points as before and those points will determine your rank.

"In the new system, besides your level and number rank, there will be a QLG. QLG stands for Quality of Life Grade, and will be in five classifications: A, B, C, D and RB, or Rank Blank. Each person will have a level rank, a QLG, followed by a number rank. For instance, an A-17 is higher than a B-2. An A-1 would be the highest overall rank in the town if that person is also in the highest level. As before, it's performance that counts. But your New Improved Number Card will do much more once the new system is totally up and running. You will also have encoded in your card, your unique identity number. No one else in the world will have the same number as you. And this number will never change for the rest of your life. It will be a rather long number, like your old Social Security number. But since that system failed even before the war, those numbers are no longer in use.

"We in ORDER are happy to announce that different countries all over the world are rapidly adopting the New Improved Number Cards and the New Improved Point System as a way to restore order to their lands. Within the next few months we expect that every country in the world will use the Point System, which we believe will usher in a new age of cooperation for us all."

"What about our old ranks?" someone shouted out.

"Yeah!" Barry muttered.

"Those ranks are invalid since the Big Boards have been down so long," Captain Sharp said.

The children began to whisper. Some groaned. But Barry waited and listened intently.

"But in reality, this is good news because each and every one of you has a chance to start over in the new order," Captain Sharp said. "If you had a poor rank before, now you have a chance to reach your full potential."

Some children clapped. Barry sat in his seat, thinking. Before Halloween, he had fallen from being Number One, but he had still been in the top twenty. He wondered where he'd rank in the new system.

Captain Sharp explained a few more of the features of the New Improved Number Cards. Then the children were dismissed. After an hour of math review, Barry's class went down to the gymnasium.

The students in the seventh grade were already in line in front of a booth which was covered with a black curtain. As the children filed in behind the curtain, Barry noticed a flash of light every few seconds, as if a camera flash was being used. Barry frowned as he watched Sloan Favor step behind the curtain.

Off to the side, Barry noticed his father and Captain Sharp talking to a group of students. Susan Kramar appeared to be arguing. Susan, a seventh-grader, was John Kramar's cousin. Barry disliked her almost as much as he did John Kramar. Amy Burke, Barry's neighbor, was also with Susan. Barry walked over to listen.

"I will not have my picture taken and put on one of those number cards and you can't make me," Susan Kramar said. "None of my friends want their picture taken either."

"Be reasonable, child," Captain Sharp said. "You're slowing down the others."

"I don't care," Susan insisted. "You don't run this town or the school. At least not yet. And there's no law which says we have to have one of those cards, is there, Mr. Smedlowe?"

"Well, there's no law . . . I guess," Mr. Smedlowe said slowly. "The Big Boards are legally allowed in school, but you don't have to participate."

"We are in a time of crisis in the world, and we have to stick together, young lady," Captain Sharp said sternly. "Your selfish attitude is unpatriotic."

"She's just a chicken Rank Blank," Barry burst out suddenly. "She knows she and her friends can't measure up. That's why she doesn't want a card."

Captain Sharp turned and smiled at Barry. Mr. Smedlowe frowned. "Barry, you stay out of this," his father said.

"I refuse to take one of those cards, and if you try and force me, I'll . . . I'll . . . sue you or the school or something," Susan said. The other students standing behind her nodded in agreement.

"I'll have to talk to the school board about this," Mr. Smedlowe said to Captain Sharp.

"Be firm, man," Captain Sharp said. "Are you going to let this . . . this little girl slow down our chances of bringing back peace and order to this town?"

"We just don't have a school policy on this issue, yet," Mr. Smedlowe said. "It was discussed before the war, but nothing was decided."

"I suggest you call a Board meeting right away," the Captain said angrily. "We in ORDER all assumed the school would demand obedience from its students."

Mr. Smedlowe looked flustered. He frowned when he saw Barry listening to their conversation. "Barry, get back in line with the others," Mr. Smedlowe said. Barry sneered at Susan and then swaggered back to the line that led behind the black curtain.

In a few minutes, Barry was holding a New Improved Number Card in his hand. The new card was thicker than the old one. A picture of Barry that almost seemed three-dimensional was on one side of the card. The other side was blank, except for a small white circle with a white X inside and the word ORDER.

Like everyone else, Barry immediately went over to the Big Board to try out the number card. But the Point System didn't seem to be working. People were gathered around in front of the long black panel discussing the problems. Normally you stuck your card into a slot on the Big Board, and after you paid a quarter, your rank appeared on the card. But all the New Improved Cards kept changing. Barry pulled his card out of the slot and was horrified to see a C-2435. But then it changed before his eyes to B-15, then to A-351, and then it changed again. The Point System was obviously still out of order. Barry was extremely disappointed.

"Why aren't these cards working?" Jason groaned.

"I don't know," Barry moaned. "Mine is all messed up too. Something is definitely wrong." Barry looked over at the kids surrounding Captain Sharp and his father. "I bet it's those Spirit Flyer kids," Barry muttered to Jason. "They could spoil everything, just like Captain Sharp said."

ORDER
CLEANS UP
· · · · · · · ·

5

On Wednesday, Barry made sure he and the other members of the Cobra Club were the first in line after school to get a Commando Patrol uniform.

The uniforms looked very similar to the ones worn by Captain Sharp and the other members of the Security Squad. They had a gray shirt, gray pants and a black belt. You were also supposed to wear black leather shoes, though most children didn't have the shoes that day in the gymnasium. Each uniform had a white circled X patch over the heart. Individual Patrol patches were worn on the left shoulder to signify the different clubs. On their right shoulder, they wore a patch that said *Centerville-M-119*. Barry had already claimed the Cobra Patrol patch for members of the Cobra Club. Sloan and his club had chosen a Super Wings bike insignia from the big book Captain Sharp had shown them. Other kids formed other patrols, usually according to their grade in school. Everyone wanted to get right to work so they would qualify for the Patrol Club that Goliath was building as an addition to the Goliath Country Club.

After an hour of sorting and changing, Captain Sharp blew his whistle. Several hundred children filled the bleachers. Many of them had already put on the gray shirt of the uniform. Captain Sharp walked up and down on the gymnasium floor in front of them. He smiled. "Peace and safety to you all," he said. He crossed his chest with both arms.

"Peace and safety," Sloan Favor and the Super Wings replied, and stood up.

"Peace and safety," Barry said, not to be outdone. The other children in the Cobra Club stood with him. They crossed their arms in the ORDER salute. Soon all the children were standing as they said the ORDER motto, their arms folded across their chests.

"You may be seated," Captain Sharp said. The children sat down obediently.

"You children are extremely fortunate to have become a part of the ORDER Youth Commando Patrol," Captain Sharp said. "All over the world, young people like yourselves are becoming part of a growing movement that will bring peace and safety to the entire world. The old is passing away and a new age of peace and safety is coming. Each one of you plays a vital part in this coming order."

Barry nodded as he listened. He was inspired by Captain Sharp's words.

"As a Commando, you are expected to live up to a high standard of citizenship," Captain Sharp said. "As we develop and expand the Commandos here in Centerville, you will learn what we expect of you and what you can expect of us. Wearing the Commando uniform means something. If you violate the honor of your uniform, you may be asked to leave the Commandos and give up the privilege of wearing the uniform."

Captain Sharp paused in his pacing. He let the words sink in as he stared at the children with his jet black eyes. His dark eyebrows made a V-shape above his nose. "As good citizens, you will learn to obey orders," the Captain said. "You will have a leader in each individual patrol. All of you will have a chance to advance in the Point System and become leaders. Each of you will have a chance to prove your loyalty, bravery, initiative and moxie as Commandos. As many of you know, some unpatriotic citizens in town want to stop the Commandos. We want to educate the Centerville community about our hopes for the future. Your assignment this afternoon is to blanket Centerville with this informative brochure."

Captain Sharp held up a colored piece of paper. He paced slowly in front of the row of bleachers. "This paper will explain what the Commandos are all about and what ORDER sees in the future, not only in Centerville, but in the state and country."

Captain Sharp walked over to a table. He picked up a shiny black plastic trash bag. He stood before the children and unfolded the plastic. *CLEAN UP! COURTESY OF ORDER* was written in large white letters on the black plastic. "Assignment number two is to pick up any trash along the streets, alleys, parks et cetera," Captain Sharp said. "ORDER wants to clean up Centerville, from the north to the south, from the east to the west. We intend to show your parents and the whole community that by working together we can make a difference and clean up this town."

Some of the children began to murmur. Barry frowned as he looked at the trash bag. Picking up trash seemed a lot like work.

"By five o'clock this afternoon, I want every person in town to have a copy of this brochure," Captain Sharp said. "I also want each of you to bring in a bag of trash. Of course, you will receive rewards for your efforts."

Captain Sharp paused. Those who had started to complain stopped. "First of all, you and your patrol will receive Good Citizen Points, which are necessary to advance in rank," the Captain said. He reached down and held up a large paperback book. "You will also receive a Commando Patrol handbook (which will explain more about the Commandos) and a copy of the Commando Patrol video tape. You will also receive free coupons to rent movie videos or video games. And finally, you will receive a new board game called The Commando Game." Captain Sharp held up a rectangular game box. Then he smiled.

"File out of here by patrols," Captain Sharp said. "There are tables set up outside with brochures and trash bags. Be good citizens and show Centerville what the Commandos are all about. I'll see you all back here at five o'clock."

Barry felt fortunate that his patrol members were nearly the first ones out the door. Men in gray uniforms stood by tables with boxes. They gave each child a stack of brochures and a trash bag.

"Can I have an extra trash bag?" Barry asked. The man smiled and gave him another. Barry, like the others, then ran for the bike racks. He hopped on his old blue bike and pedaled for the town square.

Barry parked in front of the courthouse and pushed his bike into the bike rack. He ran toward the sidewalk across the street. He thrust a brochure into the hands of a woman coming out of the shoe store. Barry then hurried to the next person, a man sitting on a bench by the music store. Barry handed out the brochures as quickly as he could. The town square was soon filled with children handing out the papers. The adults looked on in surprise. Soon, all of Barry's brochures were gone.

"I'm going to go house to house," Scott yelled out to Barry.

"Me too," Jimmy Roundhouse said. The two boys hopped onto their bikes.

Barry pulled out his first trash bag and trotted along the sidewalk picking up trash out of the gutter. He went all the way around the square. When the other children saw Barry, they began to pick up litter in the square. Both Barry and a fourth grader reached an old paper cup at the corner of Main and Tenth at the same time. Barry yanked the cup out of the smaller boy's hands.

Barry went all the way around the square and then headed south down Main Street, picking up whatever scraps of litter that he could find. By the time he got to the first houses, his sack was bulging. Barry ran back awkwardly to the square and got his bike. With great effort he rode back to the school. He was planning to turn in the first bag of trash and go for a second when he saw the kids already lining up at the tables by the gym.

Barry's face fell when he saw Sloan Favor at the front of the line. Barry couldn't believe it. Sloan had three garbage bags full of trash. By the time Barry got to the tables, Sloan and the other Super Wings members were walking away holding their Commando handbooks and other prizes.

Sloan and the other boys smiled as Barry rode by. "He just can't keep up," Sloan said out loud. Barry felt his ears turning red. He wanted to say something, but he was afraid the other boys might take away his sack of trash. Barry joined the line of children waiting to pick up their prizes.

Barry got his rewards and then raced for home. He dumped the loot in the garage and then pedaled back out into the street. Everywhere he looked, the streets and ditches were clean, as if a giant vacuum cleaner had come along and picked up every spot of litter.

Growing more frustrated by the minute, Barry had an idea. He raced over to Main Street and headed toward the town square. On each corner were garbage containers. Barry figured he could empty one and still get back over to the school with another bag of trash. But much to his dismay, the containers were empty. Either the trash had been emptied recently or someone else had the same idea. Barry wondered if that's how Sloan had filled up his three bags of trash so quickly.

Barry rode slowly home, the empty trash bag stuffed into his back pocket.

"You kids did a great job cleaning up the town this afternoon," Mr. Smedlowe said that night after supper. "That should go a long way in easing a lot of people's fears about ORDER at the meeting tonight."

"I don't see why anyone is worried about the new number cards and Commando Patrols," Barry said. "It's just those Rank Blank kids and their parents complaining because they're sore losers."

"It's not that simple," Mr. Smedlowe said. "I wish that was just the case. But it's more than children with lower ranks. Ever since the Big Boards came to town, there has been an increase in the opposition. While the Big Boards were out of operation after the war, the opposition died down. But it's not just Big Boards. It's the ORDER political party that some people don't like even though its members have become a big help to us all in such a short time. That's why I'm a member. And most of the school board is solid behind ORDER too. Captain Sharp has a good presentation prepared for tonight. I think he'll change some minds. Well, we need to leave now or be late."

As the Smedlowes were heading out of the house, the phone rang. Mr. Smedlowe answered while Barry and his mother waited in the car. When Mr. Smedlowe came outside, he had an odd expression on his face.

"Who was it?" Barry's mom asked.

"It was my brother," Mr. Smedlowe said. "He's been in some kind of trouble. He wants to send Joshua and Randy for a visit, he said, 'until it was safe,' whatever that means."

"I tried to call after we got that phone call on Sunday that sounded like Josh, but I never got through. He didn't tell you what was wrong?" Mrs. Smedlowe asked.

"He did say some things about the political situation and ORDER," Mr. Smedlowe said as he started the car. "But then the line went dead. He sounded upset. I tried to call him back, but I couldn't get through. We've got to get to the school-board meeting."

Barry thought all school-board meetings were boring. The meeting was in the school gymnasium. Chairs were set up and the bleachers pulled out. By 7:30 the place was packed. Though there were mostly adults, several children had come to the meeting also. Sloan Favor and three friends sat together wearing their new gray Commando uniforms. As soon as he saw them Barry regretted that he hadn't worn his uniform.

The school-board president introduced Captain Sharp. Several people in the audience clapped and cheered. Captain Sharp said a few words and then introduced a film similar to the one the children had seen at the school assembly. The film showed people in ORDER building new skyscrapers, making roads, putting up Big Boards in schools with neat, orderly students in classrooms, and families smiling as they worked and played together. The film ended with the people singing the national anthem in loud majestic voices.

As the lights came back on, the people in the crowd applauded loudly. Many held up signs that read *VOTE ORDER!! DECEMBER 17*. After the applause died down, Captain Sharp began to talk about ORDER and Big Boards and the Commando Patrols in the school. He also told about the New Improved Number Cards as he held one up for everyone to see. He talked about the new patriotism bringing people together all over the country within the ORDER political party. When Captain Sharp sat down, most of the audience applauded again.

Mr. Slocum, president of the school board, stood up and cleared his throat. "I think we all appreciate what ORDER has done to get this country back on its feet in this time of troubles. I appreciate ORDER, and I fully support their desire to help our young people with these patrols and these New Improved Number Cards. I want to see those new Big Boards up and working as soon as possible. I know most us have been frustrated with the Point System not working correctly."

People in the audience began clapping again with great enthusiasm. *VOTE ORDER!! DECEMBER 17* signs filled the air again. Barry watched Sloan and his friends wave the signs too.

"How does that guy do it?" Barry thought enviously. "He's always two steps ahead. I should have had a sign."

Barry wasn't paying attention, but some other people had stood up and were at the front waiting to speak. Mr. Horton, the superintendent, spoke for awhile against Big Boards and against allowing ORDER to use school property for the Commando Patrols. He talked about losing local authority to ORDER candidates. Then Sheriff Kramar was at the microphone, talking.

". . . and as a concerned parent, a patriotic citizen, and a representative of many people in this town, I want to go on record as being opposed to forcing our children to take these number cards, new or not, and being subjected to the Point System all over again," the Sheriff said. "I don't want Big Boards in our schools, and I also resent our schools being used by the ORDER political party to further their own political ends by using our children like pawns in a chess game.

"Whether our town newspaper has the courage to print it or not, there have been a number of stories about how ORDER has acted in other states since the war. Where statewide elections have already happened and ORDER has gained a majority, there have been reports that ORDER has imposed strict regulations and even resorted to abusive measures toward those people who don't support their policies. As a member of the police force, I've heard of several instances where these private ORDER Security Squads have harassed citizens. In some places, people have disappeared mysteriously. Laws have been broken and property seized without due process.

"We all realize that we are a nation in a time of emergency law, but many people can see that ORDER is taking advantage of our confusion and fear. They already practically own the banking system, not to mention having a controlling interest in many of our nation's biggest businesses. If we let them take over our schools, we are letting them go too far. Where will they stop? How much control of your lives do you want to give to them?"

Barry was surprised at the number of people who stood up and clapped in support of Sheriff Kramar. A third of the crowd seemed to agree with him.

Captain Sharp stepped quickly to the microphone. Mr. Slocum nodded, allowing him to speak.

"I would be alarmed, I suppose, if I were Sheriff Kramar and as behind in the polls as he is in the coming election," Captain Sharp said with a chuckle. He smiled and several people in the audience laughed. "But this anti-progressive attitude that he and those like him possess is responsible for the situation that led up to the most awful war in the history of this great land. The old ways and the old leadership let us down. Why should we try to turn back the clock? Do you want to go back to record inflation, unemployment and a government swamped with debt?

"If it weren't for ORDER and Goliath Industries, the Centerville Bank would have been closed and gone months ago. Where would this good town be without Goliath Industries and ORDER? Our schools are now open because ORDER and Goliath Industries were there to help. Do you want your children at home, wasting time? The Centerville young people were doing something useful and positive in the community today for the first time in a long time. With the right leadership, these young people can be organized into a powerful force for good in our world. Do you want to go back to the way things were before the war? Or do you want to go forward and pave the road into a new age of ORDER, living in peace and safety once more? I say go forward, vote ORDER!"

Many people in the crowded gym leaped to their feet in applause.

"I move we end discussion and vote," Mr. Slocum said.

"I second it," Mr. Smedlowe said.

The board voted to end discussion, and then they all stood up and left the room. In less than ten minutes they returned. Mr. Slocum stood up to the microphone.

"With respect to all opinions represented in this room and our town, the school board has decided in a five-to-two decision, which is a legal mandate, to approve the use of the New Improved Number Cards and Big Boards with our students. We strongly encourage, though we don't demand, that all students participate in using the new number cards. And finally, we feel that ORDER is helping our children, and we give them full permission to use school facilities for Commando Patrol meetings and so forth. Thank you all for coming. This meeting is adjourned."

Once more the crowd cheered. People started waving *VOTE ORDER* signs again. When Barry saw that a woman in a gray ORDER uniform was giving out signs to hold up, he ran to get one. He stood on a chair holding up the sign, cheering like everyone else.

VISITORS

· · · · · · · · ·

6

After the school-board meeting, the rest
of the week seemed dull and routine. The Big Boards were still not
working, even though they had the approval of the school board. Like
everyone else, Barry had tried the new card several times, but his rank
number kept flashing to something different every few seconds. School
work occupied most of Barry's time as with most of the other children
in Centerville. Since they had missed so much school that fall, they even
had school on Saturday of that week in order to catch up. Barry had
complained to his father, but Mr. Smedlowe said it was necessary and
that there would be more school on Saturday in the future.

Even with the extra school work, most children still went to the Commando meeting on Friday evening. All the Commando Patrols had a big party in the school gymnasium. They had free food and watched a movie about a Commando Patrol in a town which helped drive out some evil people who wanted to stop ORDER. After the meeting, Captain Sharp encouraged everyone to come to another meeting on Sunday morning. All Commandos would be going out in the town and surrounding community to encourage voter registration. Since the elections would be on Wednesday, ORDER wanted to make sure everyone had a chance to vote.

Barry woke up on Sunday morning anxious to get to the Commando meeting. He quickly put on his gray Commando Patrol uniform. He wanted to be at the meeting early to show Captain Sharp that he was a bright and eager boy.

As Barry stepped out into the hall to go downstairs, he noticed that the door to Bobby's old room was slightly open. Barry started to shut the door when he noticed them. Someone was on Bobby's bed! Barry opened the door slightly wider. Someone was also sleeping on the floor in Barry's sleeping bag. Barry backed away from the door and ran downstairs. His parents were at the kitchen table drinking coffee.

"There are people sleeping in Bobby's room," Barry announced loudly.

"Don't be so loud," Mrs. Smedlowe said softly. "It's your cousins, Josh and Randy."

"What are they doing here?" Barry demanded. "Where's Uncle Pete and Aunt Judy?"

"Josh and Randy came alone," Mr. Smedlowe said. He seemed worried. Dark splotches were under his eyes as if he hadn't slept well. "They arrived late last night."

"Well, when is Uncle Pete coming?" Barry asked. He was surprised that his father seemed so worried. "This is an odd time of year to come on vacation."

"They aren't on vacation, and I don't know when Peter is coming to pick them up, if at all," Mr. Smedlowe said. "Joshua gave me a note that Peter wrote. It doesn't sound good. Apparently, Peter and Judy are in some kind of legal trouble with the government."

"What do you mean?" Barry asked.

"I'm not sure of all the details," Mr. Smedlowe said. "I need to talk to Josh when he feels better. Both boys had fevers. They've come a long way on a hard trip."

"You'll have to talk to Josh, I guess, since Randy is such a retardo," Barry said matter of factly.

"Barry! Don't say that," Mrs. Smedlowe said with a frown.

"Well, Randy is retarded, isn't he?" Barry asked. "He even looks retarded with those big glasses and the funny way he talks."

"It's true Randy suffered some birth defects," Mrs. Smedlowe said. "His mental capacity is below average, and he's slightly retarded, but he can learn at his own pace. And he's a very nice boy."

"That's right, and we expect you to be nice to him," Mr. Smedlowe said. "After all, he may be here awhile and you need to—"

"Be here awhile?" Barry interrupted loudly. "What do you mean by that?"

"I mean that Joshua and Randy are here to live until we hear more from my brother," Mr. Smedlowe said. He took off his glasses and cleaned them with a napkin. "And since they are going to be here, your mom and I expect you to be friendly and make Josh and Randy feel at home. Do you understand?"

"Sure, as long as they stay out of my way," Barry said flatly. "And as long as Randy isn't a pest. That time we went to visit them two summers ago, he tried to tag along with us everywhere we went. He looks so dopey and dumb. It was bad enough where people didn't know you, but what will the guys in the Patrol think when they see we have a retardo, I mean . . . well, you know what I mean. We'll lose points on the Big Board for sure."

"Your friends will understand, even if the Big Board doesn't," Mrs. Smedlowe said. "Besides, the Point System isn't even working yet. And I would think you would enjoy having Josh around. He's a very capable boy. He's a good student and a good athlete. He's handsome too . . . sort of reminds me of Bobby when he was . . ."

Mrs. Smedlowe stopped. Barry was surprised. He hadn't really heard his mom mention Bobby's name in a long time. But Josh was similar to Bobby, the more Barry thought about it. Josh was twelve years old and did look like Bobby's pictures at that age. Two summers before, when they were visiting Josh's family, Barry had overheard his mother talking with his uncle and she had said that Josh looked and acted like Bobby. From that point on, Barry had looked at Josh differently. Later in that visit, Barry and Josh had been playing baseball one afternoon and Barry had almost blurted out Bobby's name when yelling at Josh to throw the ball to home plate. Barry had felt foolish, then angry. He was especially irritable at Josh the rest of their visit, though Josh hadn't done anything mean or unkind toward Barry.

"Josh can act sort of like a know-it-all, I think," Barry said. "I mean, he always acted like he was so great at everything, like sports and school."

"Well, he does have an exceptional school record," Mr. Smedlowe said. "And he's a good all-around athlete."

"That's what I mean," Barry said irritably. "He thinks he's better than everyone else. I mean, he doesn't come right out and say it, but it's more the way he acts."

"I've never seen Joshua be anything but good and kind toward you," Mrs. Smedlowe said. "I've never seen him brag or show off."

"Well, you don't know him like I do," Barry said, though as soon as he said it, he realized he didn't know Josh very well at all, especially since he hadn't seen him in two years.

"I hope your attitude changes by the time Josh and Randy wake up," Mrs. Smedlowe said. "They've been through an ordeal."

"Well, I won't bother them if they don't bother me," Barry said defiantly. "I've got to get to a meeting. Just make sure they stay out of my room, especially that Randy. He might set the place on fire or something. Don't let him play with matches or anything."

"Oh, Barry, Randy isn't like that and you know it," Mrs. Smedlowe said.

"Who knows what he'll do?" Barry asked. He walked to the door. "Maybe kids like Randy get dumber as they get older."

Barry turned his back on his mother's reply. He knew she was disagreeing, but Barry didn't want to hear. No matter what his mother or father said, having Randy around would definitely mean problems.

Barry got Napoleon and then pedaled his old blue bike to school. Bikes filled the gymnasium parking lot. Barry knocked the kickstand down, tied the dog to the rack and went inside. The first thing he noticed was a small stage set up in front of the bleachers. Behind the stage was a large Big Board hanging from wires attached to the rafters.

Alvin and Jason came over to Barry. The boys waited together on the front row of the bleachers. Little by little the rest of the Cobra Patrol came in. Sloan and his Super Wings Patrol were gathered on the top rows of the bleachers. Barry was dismayed when he realized that Sloan's Patrol seemed larger than ever. Captain Sharp started the meeting exactly at nine o'clock.

"Today you children have another chance to help improve the great town of Centerville and the surrounding community," Captain Sharp said. "As all of you know, elections will be held in this state and town on Wednesday. History will be made as ORDER is brought into our great land. This may be the most important election held in our history. Therefore, it's important that every citizen get a chance to vote. And today is the last day for voter registration. Since the regular election was canceled in November because of the confusion following the war, emergency law allows for extending voter registration to this late date. And we in ORDER want to encourage every eligible person to be a good citizen and vote. So today we are having a contest among the Commando Patrols to see which Patrol can register the greatest number of voters. Let's look at the following video to show you how to register people."

The lights went out in the gym and the Big Board lit up. The titles said *ORDER PRODUCTIONS presents VOTER REGISTRATION*. The video reminded Barry of the science movies you see in school about the importance of brushing your teeth and good nutrition. Only this film had lots of kids in it, all wearing the gray Commando Patrol uniforms. Some were in cities and some were in small towns, but they each did the same thing. They knocked on doors and talked to people, showing them the voter registration cards and smiling as they talked. After the people filled out the cards, the children gave each person a large envelope full of brochures and colorful papers about ORDER and ORDER candidates. As they left, they would check a name off the list on their clipboard and go to the next house. The whole process seemed simple enough.

There was one scene in the movie that grabbed Barry's attention. The movie showed someone refusing to talk to a boy and girl in the gray Commando uniforms. An angry man yelled at the two children. The kids in the film looked surprised that the man should be so angry. Then the camera showed an old red Spirit Flyer bike on the man's porch. The man yelled at the kids some more and threw his number card at them. The man kept yelling and acting crazy as the kids walked away.

"No wonder," one of the kids said in the video as they glanced at the Spirit Flyer. The girl looked down at her clipboard, and put a large check mark by the man's name. The two children smiled at each other and went to the next house.

After the movie was over, Captain Sharp gave them a few more instructions. An assistant handed out clipboards, larger envelopes and voter registration cards to each patrol. "Now remember, the Commando Patrol that registers the most names will receive several valuable prizes. And the Commando individual with the most names will receive fifty dollars and several coupons for free video rentals and other surprises."

Barry and the other Cobra Patrol members looked at each other eagerly.

"Most people, as you saw in the video, are patriotic, good citizens," Captain Sharp said. "But as you also noticed, there are some people who are uncooperative and troublemakers."

"Yeah, those Rank Blank Spirit Flyer people," Barry muttered. "That guy acting like a crazy man."

"Yeah," Jason said. "They're always causing trouble."

"Even if these troublemakers refuse to be good citizens, as you saw on the film, it's important to note who they are on your clipboard," the Captain said. "Just draw a red check mark by their name. It's important that we know who they are so we can try to educate them, so they can change and become good citizens. Now, I wish each patrol the best of luck. Peace and safety to you all. The contest is on, starting now!"

The children rushed out of the gym in a stampede. Barry and his friends pushed through the doors and out into the parking lot. They jumped onto their bikes and left.

Captain Sharp walked outside. A thin old man got out of a long black limousine parked near the gymnasium door. He walked over to Captain Sharp and smiled. The man looked ancient. His wrinkled skin seemed dry and worn as old leather.

"Peace and safety, Mr. Cutright," Captain Sharp saluted the old man. Mr. Cyrus Cutright crossed his chest in the same way.

The old man watched the children. With their gray uniforms on, it looked like the whole town was being invaded by an army of children. "I hear there's a meeting being planned by a lot of those Spirit Flyer people tonight," Mr. Cutright said.

"I have the situation under control," Captain Sharp said. "We'll be using some of the Commandos. I've got some eager little soldiers, especially the Favor boy and the Smedlowe boy. I'm not sure which boy to use. They both have the right qualities for the job."

"Use them both, like we've done in the past," Mr. Cutright said. "That

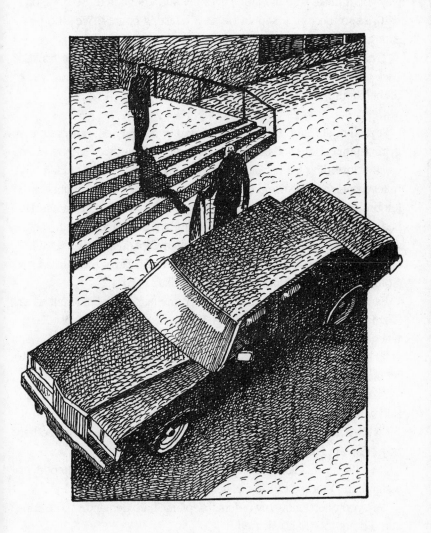

way you'll make sure the job gets done. And knowing those boys, one will rise to the top. It should be an interesting contest. We'll both be eating ashes before they're done."

"That's a great idea, sir," Captain Sharp said. Cyrus Cutright walked back to the limousine and got in. The long black car drove slowly out of the parking lot.

Several hours later, Barry and the Cobra Patrol pulled wearily into the gymnasium parking lot. Barry's face was red. His legs were rubbery and weak from riding his bicycle so much. He felt like he had ridden fifty miles that day, in town and out to the houses in the country. But he also felt proud because he had personally registered twenty-nine names. He had also put a red check mark by seven names of 'uncooperative citizens.' He had been especially pleased when Captain Sharp congratulated him on being the best of that day. Then Sloan Favor rode up on his Golden Super Wings bike. Sloan barely looked tired.

Barry stood off in the distance as Captain Sharp smiled and talked to Sloan. The older boy was smiling. Barry's heart began to sink. That's when Captain Sharp motioned for Barry to come over.

"It seems like we have a tie," Captain Sharp said. "Both of you qualify for a special top-secret assignment."

"You mean Barry and I have to work on something together," Sloan said with disgust. "But he's younger than me!"

"Well, if you don't want to accept the assignment, I could ask another boy," Captain Sharp said dryly. Sloan's eyes widened.

"No, I'll do it," Sloan said quickly. "It's just that if it's an important assignment, I thought maybe you should get someone older . . ."

"Are you questioning my orders?" Captain Sharp demanded. The Captain did not look at all pleased.

"No, sir," Sloan said quickly. "It's just that I meant that I have other guys in my patrol who I really think . . ."

Captain Sharp stared at Sloan in silence. Sloan looked down at the ground. Barry gloated inside, seeing that Sloan was in trouble.

"I'll be glad to work with Sloan, sir," Barry said with his most fake sincere voice. He had often used the same voice when trying to get out of trouble with a teacher.

"I'm glad to see at least one of you knows how to cooperate," Captain Sharp said. "Now, for the assignment. You must remember this is top secret. If you are discovered, you are in no way to say that ORDER or I myself was involved in any way. Is that understood?"

"You mean we're kind of like spies in a foreign country?" Sloan asked.

"That's one way of looking at it," Captain Sharp said. "If you are careful and do a good job, you won't have to worry. I have a simple job for you. I want you both to deliver a special package tonight."

"Deliver a package?" Barry asked. "Where do we take it?"

"As you boys discovered today, there are still many people in this town who don't want to go forward in progress in this next election," Captain Sharp said. "We have heard that a great number of these troublemakers are gathering tonight in a special meeting at the community center. You boys are simply to deliver this package after the meeting gets started and leave quietly."

"That's it?" Sloan asked. Then he smiled. "What's inside the package?"

Both boys leaned forward as Captain Sharp began to whisper. Barry's eyes widened as he listened. He smiled and then frowned.

"But couldn't we get in trouble for that?" Barry asked.

"It's only a kind of practical joke," said Captain Sharp. "But I don't expect smart boys like you to get caught."

"I won't get caught," Sloan said. His eyes looked eager and hungry. Then he glared at Barry. "Maybe this job is too hard for him, or maybe he's just chicken."

"I am not!" Barry said, making his hands into fists. "You tell me where to be and at what time, and I'll be there."

"Good," Captain Sharp said with a whisper of a smile. "I knew I could count on you boys."

NEW BIKES
ON THE BLOCK
· · · · · · · · ·

7

The rest of that afternoon Barry was nervous, thinking about the secret assignment Captain Sharp had given him. He rode around Centerville on his bike. He kept thinking of what he was going to do that night and pedaled past the community center three times. Part of Barry liked the excitement of doing something that seemed secret and dangerous. He had done a lot of things like that. Like Captain Sharp, he called them practical jokes.

Deep inside, Barry still had some doubts—not about the assignment but about Sloan Favor. No matter what the Captain said, Barry didn't trust Sloan. The older boy had made it clear he resented being stuck with

Barry. Captain Sharp must not have known Sloan and Barry hated each other, Barry had figured. But it was too late to back out. Barry had already agreed to go on the secret mission. When the sky began to get dark, Barry rode home. He pedaled up the driveway into the garage and knocked the kickstand down. He walked through the dark garage to the door that led into the house.

Inside, he heard strange voices in the kitchen. That's when Barry remembered his cousins had come to visit. Barry went into the kitchen. Both of his cousins looked about the way he remembered, only Joshua was taller. Randy still had big thick glasses and was small and runty looking, Barry thought.

"Where have you been, Barry?" Mrs. Smedlowe asked. "I thought you wouldn't get here in time to see Josh and Randy before they leave."

"Are they going home already?" Barry asked.

"No, they're going to a meeting," Mrs. Smedlowe said slowly. She wiped her hands on a dishtowel. Something about his mom's voice seemed uncertain.

"It's good to see you again, Barry," his cousin Josh said with a smile. He stepped forward and shook Barry's hand. Though Josh was twelve, he was bigger than Barry. He was also in the seventh grade. Barry couldn't help but notice the bulging muscles in Josh's arms. Josh stared at Barry's gray Commando Patrol uniform.

"Howdy, Buurrry," his cousin Randy said in his odd voice. He shook Barry's hand real hard, up and down like a pump handle. Barry pulled his hand back so Randy would stop. Randy's eyes looked tremendously big and magnified as Barry stared down at his younger cousin.

"So you guys are going to some kind of meeting?" Barry asked, stepping back away from Josh.

"Yeath," Randy said with a big smile. "I like the Flyer meetings."

"What?" Barry asked. "What are you talking about?"

Just then the doorbell rang. Barry ran to the front door. He was more than a little surprised to see John Kramar standing there.

"What do you want?" Barry demanded harshly.

"We came to pick up Josh and Randy," John said simply.

"We'll be right there," Josh said, walking up behind Barry. "Our bikes are in the garage."

Barry followed Josh and Randy out to the garage. Josh seemed to know his way around. He flipped on the light switch. Barry could hardly believe his eyes. Over on the side of the garage were two old red bicycles with big balloon tires. The words Spirit Flyer were written in flowing white letters on the middle bar. Josh rolled up the garage door. Barry kept staring at the Spirit Flyers, his mouth hanging open.

Randy ran and climbed onto his bike. The old red bicycle looked big for the little boy. Josh swung his leg over his Spirit Flyer and smiled at Barry. Barry could only stare back.

John Kramar pedaled up the driveway on his Spirit Flyer and stopped. Barry looked at him and then out to the street. Under the streetlight were several other kids on old red Spirit Flyer bicycles.

"You look like you've seen a ghost," Josh said to Barry. "You've seen Spirit Flyers before, haven't you?"

"Yeah, sure," Barry said stiffly. He swallowed. "But I didn't know you guys rode them."

"Oh, sure," Josh said with a big smile. "We've had them for quite awhile. But I wouldn't think you would be surprised. I remember the first Spirit Flyer bike I ever saw was the one Bobby rode. Do you remember him riding it?"

"Well, I don't know," Barry said, half truthfully. He remembered seeing the picture upstairs in Bobby's old scrapbook.

"I don't think he had it for long," Josh said. "He had just gotten it that summer he drowned. We have a real nice picture of him riding it in our family photo album. Of course, I didn't know how special Spirit Flyers were back then."

"Lots of people don't think those old bikes are special at all."

"Yes, I know," Josh said seriously. He looked over at John Kramar. "John's been filling me in about the situation in Centerville. He's told me a lot. And your mom told me you were helping out those ORDER people today, trying to get people to vote for them. I don't know how they got to you, but hanging around them is a big mistake."

"What do you know about anything?" Barry accused. "You just got to town, and you're already an expert about everything."

"I didn't say I was an expert about everything," Josh replied. "But I do know more about ORDER than you think. Where I live, they have taken over the whole state. They act nice on the surface, but underneath they'll do anything to get power."

"What's wrong with that?" Barry asked defensively. "The more powerful, the better. It's survival of the fittest, like they say. And besides, ORDER is here to help things run right again. You should ask my dad. He's an ORDER supporter through and through. Not like those Rank Blank Spirit . . ."

Barry stopped speaking. Joshua looked at him sadly. Randy squinted up at Barry through his big glasses.

"Is Buurrry mad at us?" Randy asked in surprise. "Why he mad?"

"Come on, Josh," John Kramar said softly. "I told you how it was."

"We're having an important meeting tonight," Josh said. "Why don't you come to it? You may learn some things. You'd be welcome."

"I'm not going anywhere with you guys," Barry said. "I want to stick with winners. The people in this town against ORDER are fighting a losing battle. Everyone knows that. If you were smart, you'd know it too."

"We better go now," John Kramar said.

"Ok," Josh said reluctantly. "We'll see you later. Let's go, Randy."

All three boys coasted down the driveway on their Spirit Flyers. Everyone in the street began pedaling their big red bikes. Barry watched them until they turned the corner. Back in the house, Barry found his mother washing dishes in the kitchen.

"Why didn't you tell me they had those old ugly Spirit Flyer bikes?" Barry asked loudly.

"I didn't know it until after you left," Mrs. Smedlowe said. She sounded worried. "When they arrived last night, your father assumed they had come on a bus to Centerville. We never dreamed they came by bicycle. I don't know how they did it."

"Who cares how they got here?" Barry exclaimed. "We can't have people with those junk-heap bikes living here. We'll be the laughing-stock of the neighborhood. Our points will drop for sure on the Big Board."

"Well, the Big Boards aren't operating yet," Mrs. Smedlowe said carefully. She seemed confused.

"Josh was also saying mean things about the ORDER party," Barry complained. "Did Dad hear him talk that way?"

"Well, he and your father did talk some this morning," his mom replied. "But I don't think they had a big discussion. Your father had to go to several meetings today. After he helped you, he went out to the Goliath Country Club."

"I can't believe they're staying at our house," Barry moaned. "They aren't even here one day and they already made friends with those Kramar kids. How did that happen?"

"They were bored after breakfast and wanted to ride their bikes around town," Mrs. Smedlowe said, hanging up the dishtowel. "That's when they told me they had traveled here on their bicycles. I still can't believe it. It's over a thousand miles. They're lucky to be alive. They lived very close to the eastern war zone."

"They must have run into John Kramar when they went riding around town," Barry said sadly, shaking his head. "Those Spirit Flyer kids all stick together. There must be fifty of them or more by now. It's like a disease that just keeps spreading."

"Those old bicycles can't be so bad," Mrs. Smedlowe said. "I never have really understood all the fuss."

"Captain Sharp says people with Spirit Flyers are troublemakers, pure and simple. They'd like to take over this town and the government."

"It's all so confusing," Mrs. Smedlowe said with a sigh. "Life used to be so simple. Even a year ago times were uncertain, but I always thought our country would pull out of it. But everything has changed so quickly. No one anticipated the confederation in Europe, and the revolutions in the Soviet Union and the changes in Japan and China." She stared off, as if looking into the past. Barry didn't like the way she was talking.

"Did Bobby ever have one of those Spirit Flyer bicycles?" Barry asked. "I thought I saw a picture of him riding one in the scrapbook."

"Yes, as a matter of fact, he did have one," Mrs. Smedlowe said. She still seemed to be looking off into the distance. "He was so excited and happy when he got it. He told your father and me all sorts of silly stories about that bike. He was so proud of it. Then he went off to camp . . ."

"What kind of stories did he tell?" Barry asked suspiciously.

"Well, I remember thinking they were very imaginative," his mom said with a smile. "He pretended he could fly on that old red bike. He said one time he escaped great danger. He said a great big snake, bigger than the county courthouse, tried to bite him, but he flew away. He really had a wonderful imagination. He was a bright child."

"Well, whatever happened to the bike?" Barry demanded. His mother frowned as she tried to remember.

"You know, I'm not really sure," she said. "I remember he took it to camp. I guess it just got left there."

Barry was going to ask another question when he noticed the big clock on the wall above the sink.

"I need to go out and see some friends," Barry said. "I'd better go."

"Who are you going to go see?"

"Just some of the guys in the club," Barry replied as he headed for the door to the garage. "We're going to study and play video games."

"Don't be out too late," Mrs. Smedlowe said. "Maybe you should take Napoleon with you."

"That worthless mutt?" Barry snorted. Ever since being attacked and hit by rocks, Napoleon had become much quieter and less willing to go out. He liked to lie on the couch and wouldn't go outside unless he was forced. Barry had taken him out some, but he had begun to hate the dog because he was such a coward. He left the dog on the couch.

Barry went to the garage. He got on his blue bike quickly and rode into the street. The night air was chilly. He pedaled over to Main, then went straight up to the town square. He turned east on Tenth Street. He saw Captain Sharp's black jeep parked in the shadow of a big oak tree in the corner of the school parking lot. Barry glided up to a stop. He frowned when he saw Sloan talking to the Captain.

"You finally got here," Sloan sneered. "I thought you had chickened out."

"Who are you calling a chicken?" Barry shot back.

"Boys, boys," Captain Sharp said. "I expect to see cooperation. Let's see the ORDER salute and motto. Commandos must be disciplined."

"Peace and safety," Barry mumbled as he crossed his arms in an X.

"Peace and safety," Sloan replied, folding and unfolding his arms quickly. Barry noticed that Sloan had been smart enough to wear his jacket.

"That's better," Captain Sharp said. He lifted a package covered with brown paper out of the front seat of the jeep. The package was in the same shape as a football, but at one end was a long coiled ball of what looked like rope or heavy string.

"This is what you boys will be delivering tonight," Captain Sharp said. He gave the odd package to Barry first. It was heavier than the boy expected.

"What is this ball of string on the end?" Barry asked.

"That's the fuse," Captain Sharp said with a smile. "And here's what you'll light it with." He held up a small disposable lighter and gave it to Sloan. "Now let me tell you the rest of the plan," the Captain said. Barry and Sloan stepped farther into the shadows to listen.

A PRACTICAL
JOKE
·········

8

Barry and Sloan rode through the darkness down the Centerville streets. The community center was near the town park in the northeast part of town. Captain Sharp had put the secret package in a large paper grocery bag and handed it to Sloan to carry. He also appointed Sloan the leader of the secret mission team. Barry was boiling with anger inside but was afraid to complain.

"Just make sure you follow my orders, and we won't mess up," Sloan whispered harshly before they had pedaled a block away from the black jeep.

"I'm not worried about me making mistakes," Barry replied quickly.

"You do your part and I'll do mine."

"I only hope you do your part right," Sloan grunted.

Barry rode in angry silence. When they reached the community center, he was surprised at the number of cars that were in the lot. Five boys crept out of the shadows of some bushes near the parking lot. Sloan waved to the boys and steered over to them. They were all members of Sloan's Super Wings Patrol.

"I wondered when you guys would get here," a boy named Robert said. He frowned at Barry. "The meeting has already started. I think most of the people have arrived. We'll be waiting for you out here."

"I thought only you and I were supposed to be doing this," Barry said to Sloan. "Why are these guys here?"

"It's really none of your business," Sloan said. "I'm the leader, and I decided I wanted some back-up help around, just in case. If it looks like there's going to be trouble, Robert is going to warn me. They also have their own mission out here in the parking lot."

"What are they going to do out here?" Barry demanded nervously. The Super Wings boys grinned and smirked as if they knew a secret. "Does Captain Sharp know they're here?"

"Barry is a sissy chicken, just like you said," Robert sneered, and nodded at Sloan. "He's so afraid, maybe he should go home and get his mama to help him."

Barry almost said something, but the way Sloan and the five other boys looked at him, Barry could tell that they were ready to fight. He was afraid, and he knew the other boys could see it.

"At least I'm not stalling or wasting time," Barry said defiantly. He got off his bike and pushed it into the row of bushes to hide it. He walked toward the community center. Sloan smiled at the other boys and then caught up with Barry.

"Keep it quiet," Sloan whispered, as they stepped inside the lobby of the building. They walked quickly up the stairs that led to the small balcony. Sloan used a key that Captain Sharp had given him to unlock the balcony door. After they were inside, they closed the door quietly.

"We wait until I say so to set off the bomb," Sloan whispered. Barry nodded. Both boys crouched down and peeked over the railing at the meeting down below. It was easy to hear and see what was going on.

Barry had never seen such a sight. The room was filled with Spirit Flyer bicycles. People were sitting in chairs next to their bikes. Barry didn't think it was possible that so many of the old red bikes could have been in Centerville without him noticing it. Many of the bikes belonged to the adults.

"We're supposed to wait until they start arguing," Sloan whispered to Barry. "Even if the time is right, we wait until then."

"But how does Captain Sharp know they'll argue?" Barry asked. Sloan shrugged impatiently.

Josh, Randy and John Kramar were all on one side of the room sitting with most of the other children. Mr. Fenly, who owned one of the gas stations in town, was talking. "I say we shouldn't be so upset about these upcoming elections. Though I don't agree with everything Goliath and ORDER have done, no one can deny that they've given people good jobs. People have to make a living.

"Now, I like my Spirit Flyer as well as anyone, and I don't particularly care for the way the Point System works, but I think we can all work out our differences. That's what made this country great; people can have different points of view and still get along together. I think we should try to compromise and live with each other. I don't see why we can't use the number cards like they say and still think and believe what we want. After all, this country has been through a sad, confusing time. We need to stick together. I've been reading some of the things ORDER has been saying, and I think they make a lot of sense on some issues, especially when it gets down to dollars and cents, which is something we all need—money."

Barry was surprised when a good portion of the adults began to clap in approval. Sheriff Kramar stood up to speak. He stood between an old red Spirit Flyer and his deputy, George, who sat in a wheelchair. Next to George sat an old man with white hair that Barry didn't recognize as being from Centerville. Sheriff Kramar cleared his throat.

"I'm the first to admit that business and dollars and cents are important. And no one can deny that Goliath and ORDER have created jobs in Centerville and kept people working. Money is important, but my question is, what is all this going to cost us in the long run? As Sheriff, I get reports from all over the state and even the nation, and I tell you, there have been too many reports in too many places of ORDER or Goliath Industries abusing their power. Those states nearest the war zones are in real trouble. Mr. Chuck Peek and Mr. Steve Penn, attorneys at the law firm of Peek and Penn, have heard terrible reports from their lawyer friends in other states. People are in jail without due process of the law. People have disappeared. They say people have even died suspiciously. A lot of local law-enforcement agencies have been crushed by this martial law and the power has been handed over to those in the private ORDER Security Squads."

"But those Security Squads get the job done," Mr. Crenshaw said, as he stood up. He owned the hardware store. "I see it on the TV news every night. Those ORDER Security Squads have kept those rowdy gangs under control. Right after the war, some cities were practically under siege by gangs from the way it looked on the TV. There was looting and burning. Food markets were attacked and emptied out within hours. Until those ORDER boys came in and busted a few heads, things were out of control. And I for one don't want my store broken into and looted. I agree with Jim Fenly. Goliath and ORDER have been good for business. Maybe you're just worried about your job, Bill. These local police are upset just because the federal government has gone over their heads."

Some people in the audience nodded and smiled. Sheriff Kramar looked flustered. "I admit, I don't like other government agencies coming into Centerville and telling me how to do my job," Sheriff Kramar said. "But I've tried to cooperate as well as I can and keep my integrity.

But I'm telling you, these Security Squads cut too many corners. Just over in Adair County, the jails are full of people arrested under unusual circumstances. The Security Squad forces are for all practical purposes running the town."

"That's hogwash and rumors," Mr. Crenshaw said. "If that was happening, why haven't I seen it on the TV news? Those TV men would be on a story like that like a dog on a bone."

"But since the war, news organizations have been under strict martial law like everyone else," Sheriff Kramar said. "They have to answer to government censors now. And besides that, the biggest news organizations belong to corporations owned by Goliath Industries or belong to ORDER-related groups. Many of the big businesses who advertise are also linked with ORDER. Have you ever seen a negative report on either ORDER or a Goliath Industries company? I haven't."

People began to murmur and talk. Barry watched as they shook their heads. According to the clock, they still had at least fifteen minutes to go before setting off the bomb.

"I still say we can live with ORDER if we have to," Mr. Fenly said as he stood back up. "I don't want to vote for them, but if they win, and it looks like they've got a good chance, we can't just all move out of the country. We can still believe what we want. They may call us names because we like Spirit Flyer bicycles, but what does a name hurt?"

It can hurt plenty, Barry thought to himself. He didn't see how anyone would want to be Rank Blank.

"Maybe we've been too critical about the Big Boards and Point system, too," Mr. Fenly continued.

"But you've never been called a Rank Blank," John Kramar said suddenly, standing up. "I think the Point System stinks. And it's not part of the kingdom. I thought this meeting was to talk about the Three Kings and Spirit Flyers and all the ways we can fight back. In *The Book of the Kings* it says we should resist evil."

The kids in the audience clapped their hands. John looked embarrassed and sat back down. Mr. Fenly looked annoyed because he had been interrupted.

"Don't try to tell me about Spirit Flyers, young man," Mr. Fenly said. "I've had a Spirit Flyer since before you were born, and I want you to notice the condition of my bike." Mr. Fenly pointed down at his old red bicycle. He smiled with pride. "Do you see the shine on this bicycle?" Mr. Fenly asked. "As a member of Eastside Spirit Flyer Club, we have gotten together every month to polish and work on these bikes. Look at that chrome shine! And there's not a bit of rust on that chain."

Mr. Brown, a machinist out at the Goliath factory stood up to speak. He smiled down at his bike. "Now this bike of mine is really something special," Mr. Brown said. "I'm glad we're starting to talk about bikes instead of all this politics stuff. I don't think Spirit Flyer meetings should get into politics. Bikes are bikes and politics are politics, and they don't mix. As most of you know, I'm a member of the United Wheels, USA Spirit Flyer Club that meets over in Kirksville. We've got one of the best collections of Spirit Flyers in the state. We have strict standards. To qualify, you have to have all original instruments properly placed on your bike. You have to come faithfully to each meeting each weekend. Our club won several perfect attendance awards and bicycle safety awards. I tell you, when you get all those bikes together, sitting there, all shiny and greased up, it does something to you right here." Mr. Brown tapped his chest above his heart.

As he sat down, Mrs. Johnson stood up. She smiled and nodded at everyone. "I've had my Spirit Flyer since I was in college," she said proudly. "Everyone tells me my Spirit Flyer looks in great shape. As you can probably tell, it has very low mileage. I've tried to be extra careful with it. I'm a member of the Kingdom Klub, which meets in the south part of town. I'm also president this year of the Tuesday Morning Flying Wheels meetings. We have some of the most lively discussions you can imagine about Spirit Flyers." She sat down and the people applauded.

Another man, Mr. Jones, a carpenter, stood up near Mr. Fenly. "I think it's really great that we can all get together like this, even though many of us are in different Spirit Flyer clubs in Centerville and the local area. It thrills me to see all these bikes, shiny and polished. Like many of you, I've been saddened that we don't get together like this more often. Locally, I belong to the King's Book Club. As most of you know, we put a priority on knowing the manual, *The Book of the Kings.* We believe that if you're going to know about the bikes, you have to know that manual, frontward and backward. I can understand what Mrs. Johnson is saying about good discussions. I've been in club meetings until two in the morning where we got to arguing . . . I mean, discussing some of the finer points, especially on the mechanics of the bikes. But you got to know the manual.

"Some of the old-timers in our club have whole chapters memorized. They could take apart a Spirit Flyer and put it back together with their eyes closed. They know where each instrument goes. And they also know which ones are for decoration and which ones are really meant to be used. That's where a lot of these less-informed clubs go wrong."

"Now wait a minute!" said another man who stood up. He wore glasses and looked nervous. Barry didn't recognize him. "From what you just said, you're implying that some of the instruments actually work when it's common knowledge that they are broken. We must remember to see Spirit Flyers in their historical perspective. The instruments are reminders of what the kings once did, or may have done. You can't believe an old broken horn is meant to work in today's modern age."

"What I don't understand is these people who insist that the bikes are to be ridden at all," a woman named Mrs. Garner said as she stood up. "I don't think the kings meant for us to really ride them. They're so old and rickety, it's embarrassing and dangerous both. In our club, we see them as symbols that show we belong to the kings."

"In our club we ride them," Mr. Jones said. "But we only ride them on Sundays. We make sure we don't ride them out in public where others can see us. We don't want to confuse other people."

"You're just ashamed to be seen on them, I think," someone said.

"That's not true," Mr. Jones said angrily. "But I do think we have a responsibility to keep our reputation. After all, if we confuse others in the wrong way, they may think we're foolish for riding them in public."

"Well, in our club we ride them," the man with the glasses said. "But only on special days during the year."

"That's not the way it's supposed to be done," said a young woman. "Everyone knows you ride a Spirit Flyer when you first receive it. Then you keep it as a reminder of the kings and the kingdom. Riding it once is enough."

"But what good is a bicycle if you don't ride it?" John Kramar asked loudly as he leaped to his feet.

The old man sitting next to Sheriff Kramar stood up. He patted John on the back. "I think the boy is right," the old man said. "What good is a Spirit Flyer bicycle if it's not ridden?"

There was a moment of silence in the room. Suddenly, there were several people all trying to talk at once down on the floor below. Barry was surprised. He could only understand snatches of words. Both he and Sloan kept watching the big clock at the front of the room. Sloan turned the bomb in his hand.

Barry didn't understand what all the fuss was about. Some people were arguing about whether to ride or not while others were arguing about horns and lights and gear shifts. Still others were opening books and pointing at the pages, apparently trying to prove their side of an argument. Just like Captain Sharp had predicted, the Spirit Flyer people were arguing among themselves. Some were even getting angry.

"It's time," Sloan said. He turned the bomb carefully in his hands. "I'll go downstairs to yell and confuse them. Light the fuse in exactly one minute. Then get out."

"That's not the way Captain Sharp said to do it," Barry hissed.

"I'm the leader," Sloan said, handing Barry the lighter. "Light it in one minute."

Barry put the bomb down in the front aisle of the balcony. He was glad all the people were yelling and talking. Then he watched the clock, counting the seconds. With thirty seconds remaining, John Kramar looked around the room nervously.

"The horn is blowing!" John yelled. "It's a warning!"

"I hear it too," Josh Smedlowe said. "It is a warning. The kings are trying to tell us something."

The room was silent for a second. People cocked their heads as if trying to listen. Barry began to sweat. He couldn't hear a thing.

"I don't hear anything," the young man with glasses said. "As I said, none of these instruments are meant to work today, they are only . . ."

The people began to argue once more. Barry smiled and lit the fuse. He was surprised how fast the fuse burned and sputtered.

Barry scurried for the balcony door. He pushed against the door and turned the knob at the same time. But the door didn't budge. He turned it again. He pushed and shoved. The door was stuck. Barry looked over at the bomb. He thought about trying to jump over the balcony.

The bomb popped like a firecracker. Then smoke began pouring out in an angry black cloud. People began to yell and scream. In seconds the smoke had filled the balcony and was rapidly filling the rest of the large room. Barry pounded on the door. He began to cough as the smoke covered him. He was sure he would suffocate when the door suddenly opened. Barry fell forward into the hall.

Sheriff Kramar helped Barry to his feet. While some other men rushed into the balcony with a fire extinguisher, Sheriff Kramar led Barry downstairs. Barry was still coughing when they got outside. The parking lot was filled with people and Spirit Flyer bicycles. Many people were coughing; some were rubbing their red wet eyes. Josh and Randy stood by an old pickup truck with flat tires. They stared with surprise at Barry.

"We need to have a talk, young man," Sheriff Kramar said. Barry looked up into the Sheriff's serious eyes. In the distance, Barry could hear the sound of fire engines coming closer.

THE LOCKER
ROOM FIGHT
· · · · · · · ·

9

Barry got to school late the next morning. He had just come from the Sheriff's office with his father. Once Barry had finally admitted to setting off the bomb that night, Sheriff Kramar had sent him home with his parents. For a while, Barry had been afraid he would actually have to spend the night in jail. Barry woke up, hoping it had all been a bad dream. But then he smelled his smoky clothes lying on the floor. They were gray with soot.

The night before, while men from the fire department cleared the smoke out of the community center, Captain Sharp had driven up in his black jeep. Several other men from the Security Squad had shown up behind him in another black jeep. When Sheriff Kramar was busy talking to the fire fighters, Captain Sharp had walked over to Barry.

"Listen carefully, my boy," Captain Sharp had hissed as he whispered. "You are not to implicate anyone else in this blunder of yours, or else you will regret it. Do you understand me?"

"But Sloan locked me in the balcony," Barry had blurted out, tears filling his eyes.

"That's not how I understand what happened," Captain Sharp had replied. "But we can worry about that later. The point is, you got caught. So you must be clear in telling them that you acted alone and on your own. We can't have people thinking ORDER was involved in something like this right before the elections."

"But I'll get in real trouble," Barry had whimpered.

"You are already in real trouble," Captain Sharp had said. "But there are ways to deal with this. I'll see what I can do to delay things. After the elections on Wednesday, this regrettable incident will blow away like smoke. But you must not implicate your friends in this matter. Am I making myself clear?"

Barry had only nodded. Captain Sharp got in his black jeep and drove off. Soon afterward, Mr. Smedlowe took Barry home.

Barry and his father went to the Sheriff's office that morning. Sheriff Kramar asked Barry all sorts of questions, and Barry lied in most of his answers. Besides the smoke bomb, most of the cars in the parking lot had flat tires because the air had been let out. Barry had sworn he knew nothing about the flat tires. He lied, saying he made the bomb himself from leftover firecracker and smoke bombs from the Fourth of July. He pretended that he didn't know it would make so much smoke. Mr. Smedlowe had agreed to pay for the damages to the community center. One of the seats in the balcony had been ruined. The janitor down at the community center was also going to charge for cleaning up the place from the smoke and soot. But the worst thing was that Barry would have to see a judge later that month.

Mr. Smedlowe was still angry as they drove from the Sheriff's office to the school. He parked his car in the principal's parking space but didn't get out. He stared at Barry. "I don't know what's gotten into you, Barry," Mr. Smedlowe said. He took off his glasses and cleaned them. "I realize you don't like those people with Spirit Flyers, but why would you pull a stupid prank like that? What if the whole building had caught on fire? How could you do such a thing?"

Barry remained silent, slumped down in his seat. His father had been asking those same questions the night before and all that morning. No matter what Barry said, his father wasn't satisfied. So Barry said nothing, hoping he could just go to class.

"I just don't understand it," his father muttered. "When Bobby was your age, he never caused us a lick of trouble. Not a lick."

Barry's jaw clenched at the sound of Bobby's name. He absolutely hated it when his father brought up Bobby. You would have thought Bobby was perfect, the perfect ghost. Barry was ready to scream by the time his father got out of the car. The school bells were ringing.

"Now go straight to class and see if you can stay out of trouble," Mr. Smedlowe said. Barry nodded and left.

As Barry walked into the school, he saw by the clock that it was already time to go to gym class. He walked down the hall to the locker room. Everyone was busy changing into their gym shorts. Barry walked down the aisle of lockers. The seventh graders were just leaving. Only they hadn't all left.

"Let go. Let go," said a vaguely familiar voice. Barry passed the next row of lockers. Sloan Favor and several other guys in his club were crowded together. Sloan turned slightly and smiled when he saw Barry.

"Hey, I heard you got caught smoking last night down at the community center," Sloan said chuckling. "Little boys like you shouldn't play with matches."

The other Super Wings guys began to laugh too. Barry was about to say something when he saw a large pair of glasses on a small boy. "Let go me. Let go," the boy said. He lunged forward but Sloan and the other boys caught him. That's when Barry saw that they had Randy. The little boy struggled to get free. Fear was all over his face. When he looked at Barry through his thick glasses, he reminded Barry of a small frightened rabbit.

"Hey, you guys, leave Randy alone," Barry said. "He's my cousin."

"I might have figured you'd have a retardo for a cousin," Sloan said. "It must run in your whole stupid family."

The other boys laughed. Randy struggled to get away. His big eyes blinked.

"Randy the Retardo Smedlowe," Sloan said. "Kind of rhymes, doesn't it? Randy the Retardo Smedlowe. He's one of those Rank Blank Spirit Flyer kids. I saw him leave your house this morning on one of those ugly old bikes. Randy the Rank Blank Retardo Smedlowe. I like that name the best."

"Leave him alone," Barry said nervously. "He hasn't done anything to you guys."

"I'm not so sure about that," Sloan said. "He was sneaking around these lockers. I think he was trying to steal something. Were you trying to steal something from my locker?"

Sloan shook Randy. The little boy's glasses slid down his nose. "Not stealing," Randy stammered. "Not . . ."

Barry could tell that Randy was about to cry. Some other kids had gathered behind Barry. They were ready to watch the fun.

"Go ahead, Sloan," someone shouted. "Coach is out in the gym."

"Does Randy the Retardo want to snoop around lockers?" Sloan said. The boys began to laugh. Sloan then jerked Randy over to the wall of lockers. "Open up a locker, Skeeter."

A boy next to Sloan pulled open a locker. Sloan dragged Randy over to it. The little boy was muttering and talking softly.

"What did you say, Randy?" Sloan demanded. He shook the boy. Randy just kept muttering.

"I can't hear you." Sloan leaned forward, listening, a bitter smile was on his face. "What are you talking about, Randy? There aren't any kings around here." Sloan looked at the other boys. "You guys see any kings around here? This little runt has really flipped out. He's talking nonsense to himself. We better put him in the locker until he settles down. He might be dangerous."

"Yeah, we wouldn't want him to hurt anyone," Skeeter said. Sloan jerked Randy over to the open locker. He started to push him inside but Randy began to squirm.

"Stop it," Barry said. "He's just a little kid."

"You sticking up for your Rank Blank relative, Smedlowe?" Sloan demanded. Randy kept struggling. His glasses fell down on the concrete floor. Skeeter picked them up and tossed them in the open locker. "So what if he is a retardo," Barry said, smiling nervously, trying to act like he agreed with Sloan. "You might as well let him go."

"Are you going to make me?" Sloan said. He pushed Randy all the way inside the locker. When he slammed the door shut, all the guys cheered.

"Let me out. Let out," Randy screamed from inside the locker, banging on the metal. The boys laughed again. Just then, Josh Smedlowe pushed through the crowd.

"What's going on?" Josh demanded when he saw Barry. "I heard someone was picking on my brother. Where is he?"

"Let out! Let out!" Randy yelled from inside the locker. The metal banged. Josh frowned as he looked at the locker. Sloan folded both arms across his chest and smiled at Josh.

"Are you letting them hurt Randy?" Josh asked Barry.

"I didn't do anything," Barry said.

"Yeah, I can see that," Josh replied with disgust. He walked over to the locker. As he reached out to open it, Sloan grabbed his hand.

"What do you think you're doing?" Sloan asked.

"I'm letting my brother out," Josh said. Josh shook off Sloan's hand.

But Sloan quickly stepped in front of the locker.

"So Randy the Rank Blank Retardo Smedlowe is your brother?" Sloan asked. The other boys laughed.

"Yes, he is and I'm letting him out," Josh said firmly. "Now move out of my way."

Josh reached over to the locker handle. But Sloan knocked his arm away in a karate chop.

"I don't want trouble," Josh said. "But I'm going to let my brother out."

Josh moved toward the locker again, but Sloan suddenly shoved him backward. While Josh was off balance, Sloan swung a fist right for his face. At the last instant, Josh ducked and swung back, hitting Sloan on the side of the head. Barry was surprised at the way the seventh grader's head snapped back from the blow. Sloan fell backward and crashed into the lockers at the back of the aisle. He then slid down to the floor. His eyes looked dazed and confused.

"Did you see that?" someone whispered.

"What a punch!"

Josh took a deep breath, walked over to the locker and opened it. Randy was shaking as he got out. Josh reached down and gave the little boy his glasses. Randy looked up at Josh quietly.

"You stick with me," Josh said softly.

Just then Sloan came out of his daze. He struggled to his feet. "You asked for it," Sloan yelled as he lunged at Josh. Barry could hardly believe what happened next because it happened so fast. As Sloan charged, Josh stepped slightly to one side. He grabbed Sloan's arm and twisted it, then jerked back. Sloan flipped completely over and landed on the hard floor with a thud. For an instant there was silence, Sloan shook his head, trying to figure out how he got on the floor. He gasped for air as he glared up at Josh.

"Get him!" Sloan hissed to his friends. In an instant the other boys in the Super Wings rushed toward Josh. Josh sprang into action. He knocked down the first three boys. But then Sloan grabbed his legs and Josh fell. The other boys were on him.

"Stop hurt my bruddder!" Randy screamed. "Stop hurt him."

"Barry, help!" Josh yelled, looking out from under the pile. But Barry could only stare. He felt paralyzed with fear as he saw more Super Wings guys jump into the battle. Barry was going to run for help to the coach, when John Kramar and Daniel Bayley pushed past him. They pulled three guys off Josh. Then some other guys went in to help John and Daniel.

That's when the whistle blew. As quickly as it had started, it stopped. By the time Coach Goober had pushed his way through the crowd of boys, Josh and Sloan were back on their feet. Sloan had a trickle of blood running out of his nose. Josh's face was red, but he seemed ok.

"Break it up! Break it up!" Coach Goober yelled. "What's going on here?"

"Nothing," Sloan said, wiping the blood off his face with his sleeve. Coach Goober looked at all the boys suspiciously.

"You boys want to fight, do it after school," the coach said with disgust. "Now all of you, get where you're supposed to be. Fast."

"You in on this, Smedlowe?" the coach asked Barry.

"I was just standing here," Barry blurted out defensively. "I didn't do anything."

"He's certainly right about that," Josh muttered. He stared at Barry with disgust. Then he looked at John and Daniel. "Thanks, guys."

John and Daniel just nodded. They all looked at Barry in silence. Barry felt his face turning red. He pushed through the crowd and walked to his locker. He changed into his gym shorts as fast as he could. In the next aisle he could hear the other boys talking.

"Did you see how that new kid could punch?" someone said.

"He must know karate or something the way he flipped Sloan."

Barry left the locker room quickly.

THE CLUBHOUSE JAILBREAK

• • • • • • • • •

10

All that morning Barry wished he could leave school, but he knew he couldn't. All day long he heard about the fight in the locker room. He also heard the other kids whispering about him and the smoke bomb at the community center. It seemed like everyone knew that Barry had set off the smoke bomb, that he had a cousin who knew how to fight and that he also had a cousin who was retarded. He also heard other things. He heard some boys saying that Josh had asked Barry to help him in the fight but that Barry had chickened out. Barry felt miserable. He knew he had to do something. During his social-studies class, Barry had an idea.

In the break after lunch, Barry called a quick meeting of the Cobra Patrol. All the members gathered together by the dugout at the baseball field. But before the meeting could even start, some of the boys were whispering and grinning as they looked at Barry. When Roger Darrow started to laugh out loud, Barry frowned.

"Who are you laughing at?" Barry demanded.

"Don't be such a hothead," Jason said.

"Yeah," Roger added. "If you get too hot, you might catch on fire and start smoking."

Without a word, Barry lunged forward and pushed Roger backward. Roger tripped on the dugout bench and fell backward into the dirt. The other kids in the patrol stared silently at Barry.

"Well, he deserved it," Barry said angrily. "No one makes fun of me and gets away with it."

They all looked at Barry in stony silence. Roger slowly got back up to his feet. He dusted himself off.

"Is it true that little retardo kid is your cousin and he's living at your house?" Jason asked.

"Well, sort of," Barry said. "But it wasn't like I invited them to come. They just showed up."

"They both have those Rank Blank old bikes," Freddie said coldly.

"Well, I didn't call this meeting to talk about my stupid Rank Blank cousins," Barry said. He smiled, but no one smiled back.

"Did you really get caught last night trying to burn down the community center?" Roger Darrow asked.

"I wasn't trying to burn down anything," Barry whined. "It was just a little smoke bomb. But I don't want to talk about that either."

"My mom was sure talking about it," Alvin said. "My mom was talking to me about you this morning. She was saying I probably shouldn't be hanging around you. She said you'd get us all in trouble."

"My parents said stuff like that too," Freddie added.

Some of the other kids nodded as they looked at each other.

"No one's going to get you in trouble," Barry said loudly. "In fact, I'm not in any real trouble. It was all a big misunderstanding."

"That's not what I heard," Alvin said, shaking his head.

"Yeah, Sloan Favor said you'd probably end up in jail or one of those reform schools," Jason added.

"Sloan Favor is a dirty liar! You guys should know that by now," Barry said angrily.

"I'd like to see you say that to his face," Roger Darrow said softly. "Of course, you had your chance to fight him this morning in gym class, but you didn't."

Barry almost lunged at Roger again, but he stopped himself. His hands were in fists. Nothing about the meeting was going the way he expected.

"Look, I intend to get even with Sloan Favor," Barry said calmly. "And I'm going to do it this afternoon when we get our clubhouse back."

"Get our clubhouse back?" Jason asked. "How are you going to do that?"

"I've got a plan," Barry said.

"But he has a padlock on it and everything," Roger replied.

"Well, I've got a hacksaw at home that will do the job," Barry answered. "But we have to stick together. Now, do you guys want to get our clubhouse back or not?"

"Sure," Alvin said. The others all nodded their heads though they didn't look too confident.

"Then listen carefully," Barry said. "We've got to make sure this is kept an absolute secret."

Barry frowned as he looked at each face in the group. The other boys looked uneasy somehow. Barry wondered if they were scared.

"We're going to get it back right after school today," Barry said. "They'll probably be out running errands for Captain Sharp. And while they're doing that, we'll get our clubhouse and put our own lock on it."

"Sounds kind of sneaky to me," Roger said slowly. "I thought you said you were going to fight Sloan over it."

"I'll take care of Sloan when I'm good and ready," Barry said. "Are you sure you aren't just chicken?"

"I'm no chicken," Roger said. Barry could tell Roger was angry.

"Good, then listen up," Barry replied. "Here's the plan."

The club crowded in around their leader. As Barry explained the plan, he began to feel better. With his club behind him, Barry was sure everything would be all right.

Barry felt better after telling his club about his plan to get back the clubhouse, but being in school the rest of that Monday was hard. Everywhere Barry went, he saw kids whispering and giggling about him, or at least he imagined they were talking about him. When the last bell rang, Barry bolted out of the school.

Since he didn't have his bike that day, he ran all the way home. He was huffing and puffing by the time he opened the garage door but that didn't slow him down. His father's tools were on shelves at the front of the garage. Barry got the hacksaw, hopped on his old blue bike and pedaled down the driveway.

Just as he had planned, the Cobra Patrol had gathered at the old gazebo by the courthouse in the town square. They seemed oddly silent as Barry rode up. They all had their jackets zipped all the way up to their collars, which Barry thought was odd since it wasn't that cool outside.

"What's up?" Barry asked. He was still breathing hard. "You guys aren't chickening out, are you?"

No one said anything. Barry looked from face to face. Finally Roger Darrow thumped Barry on the back.

"We're here, aren't we?" Roger said. "Let's go give Sloan Favor what he deserves."

"And we'll get what we deserve, right?" Barry asked. "Follow me."

Barry started pedaling away from the gazebo. The other boys followed but at a distance. Barry crossed the street and then rode into the alley. The other boys crossed the street slowly on their bikes.

The alley was clear. Barry picked up speed as he got closer to the clubhouse. The padlock was locked on the door. When Barry was sure no one was inside, he parked his bike. He looked up and was surprised to see that his club members were still down at one end of the alley.

"Come on and help me," Barry yelled. He took the hacksaw and began pushing and pulling it over the lock. A little dent appeared in the metal and Barry sawed faster. Out of the corner of his eye he saw bicycle tires roll up.

"It's about time you guys got here," Barry muttered. He looked up. Sloan Favor was sitting on his bike, his arms folded across his chest. Sloan was wearing his gray Commando Patrol uniform. He had a wicked smile on his face. All around Sloan were members of the Super Wings Patrol. Barry looked frantically down the alley. The Cobra Patrol guys were riding slowly toward Sloan and the others. Barry figured it would be about three to one if they started to fight since Sloan's Patrol was so much bigger.

"What do you think you're doing, Smedlowe?" Sloan asked.

"I'm taking back what's mine," Barry said nervously. He felt a little better as the guys in the Cobra Patrol rolled up and stopped. "This was our clubhouse and you stole it. I'm just taking it back for me and my patrol."

"Do you have a patrol?" Sloan asked. "Who's in it?"

Barry frowned at Sloan. The older boy acted like he knew something Barry didn't.

"Of course I have a patrol," Barry said. He turned to the guys in the Cobra Patrol and nodded. "It looks like we may have to fight this thief."

Sloan looked around the group. Then he smiled at Barry. "I don't see any thief but you," Sloan said. "And I don't see any patrol but mine. Are any of you guys in this thief's patrol?"

Sloan looked around the group once more. No one moved. Barry stared at the guys in his patrol. Roger Darrow grinned just like Sloan. "I don't see anyone that belongs to his patrol," Roger said. The rest of the boys that had been in the Cobra Patrol nodded.

"Come on, you guys," Barry said. "We can fight these guys. Let's get our clubhouse back."

"We have a clubhouse," Alvin said. "And you were trying to break into it."

The guys in the old Cobra Patrol unzipped their jackets. Barry's eyes went wide when he saw the bottles and rocks. Sloan grinned.

"You've been a bad boy, Barry," Sloan said, shaking his head. "Last night you tried to burn down the community center, and today you're a thief trying to break into our clubhouse. I think you need to be punished. That's what happens to lawbreakers and thieves."

Barry began to sweat as the other kids stepped closer. They moved slowly around him in a semicircle, closing off any way to escape.

"Hey, come on, guys! This isn't fair!" Barry said.

"Do you deny you were trying to steal this clubhouse?" Sloan asked.

"Well, I was just . . . you know," Barry said. His voice cracked. He sounded as if he were about to cry. Sloan grinned wickedly. He nodded at two boys next to him. The seventh-grade boys got off their bikes.

Barry tried to run, but two seventh graders caught him and yanked his arms behind his back. Barry struggled and pulled, but it was useless. Sloan got off his bike. He walked slowly over to Barry.

"I heard you say you were going to fight me," Sloan said.

"I didn't say that," Barry yelped.

"Yes, he did," Roger Darrow said. "We all heard him this afternoon."

Sloan looked at Barry and smiled again. Then he spit right in Barry's face. All the other boys began to laugh.

"Let's fight," Sloan said. He suddenly punched Barry in the stomach.

"Ugggggghhh," Barry grunted, his knees buckling. He felt like he could hardly breathe. His eyes were watery and blurry. He was sagging so much, his knees almost touched the ground.

"You know, we could use Barry for a punching bag," Sloan said. "But I have a better idea."

Sloan walked over to the clubhouse and unlocked the padlock with a key. He opened the door. He walked back to Barry.

"You wanted the clubhouse, so I think you can have it for a while," Sloan said. "Put him inside."

The two older boys dragged Barry to the clubhouse and pushed him inside. Barry hit the wooden floor of the shed with a thump. Sloan slammed the door shut, put on the padlock and locked it.

"Barry's in jail," Roger said with glee.

"That's what happens to bad boys like Barry," Sloan announced to the group. "Thieves and firebugs end up in jail."

The kids in the alley began laughing and joking. Some pounded on the sides of the clubhouse. Others threw rocks up on the roof.

"I hear that Barry likes smoke bombs," Sloan said. "And I just happen to have some."

Inside the dark walls, Barry heard some of the boys leaving. Though his stomach ached, he stood and looked desperately around the small wooden shed. There were no windows, and only cracks between the boards let light in. When Barry's club had possession of the little shed, Barry had kept candles and an old kerosene lantern for light, but now the little shack was empty except for an old wooden crate. The place was quite dark. Outside, the other boys kept yelling and pounding on the walls. Barry was on the verge of tears. His stomach hurt. Sloan stuck his face up to a board with a knothole.

"Barry, are you in jail?" Sloan asked. "I've got something for you."

There was a pause. Then Sloan pushed a round marble-sized object through the knothole. It fell to the floor in a sizzle. Barry ran to the opposite side of the clubhouse and put his hands over his ears. Instead of exploding, it began to spew out smoke. Three more of the little smoke bombs fell into the shack. Barry began to cough and his eyes watered. He heard more smoke bombs falling onto the floor, but he couldn't see them, the place was so filled with smoke.

"Let me out!" Barry screamed. "I can't breathe."

Barry pounded on the walls. He tripped over the wooden crate. As he got back up, he saw a crack of light at the top of the back wall of the clubhouse. He moved the crate over and stuck his nose up to the crack. For an instant, he could breath fresh air. He hit the wall with his fist. The old rotten wood splintered, leaving a hole almost as big as his face. He stuck his head out. There was a gap a foot and a half wide between the back wall of the clubhouse and the brick wall of the toy store. Barry pulled on the board and it splintered and cracked halfway down the wall. He pulled the next board and it broke. Barry stepped up into the gap. He turned sideways and pulled himself out into fresh air. He was going to hop down and run for it when he heard a shout.

"He's getting out the back!" someone yelled. Immediately, both escape routes were blocked. That's when Barry looked up. Right above him was an old rusty drainpipe. Barry grabbed it. He pulled himself up, stepping on an old window ledge. Then he put one leg on the roof of the clubhouse.

"He's going up on the roof," someone yelled. Barry didn't look back. He grabbed the drainpipe, climbed up a few more feet and grabbed the edge of the roof of the toy store. As he pulled himself up, a rock thudded into his back. He pulled himself over onto the roof.

"Get him!" Sloan yelled. The boys started giving each other hands up so they could get on top of the clubhouse roof. Two boys grabbed onto the old drain pipe and started to climb to the top. But the old pipe suddenly bent and gave way. Both boys jumped back on the roof of the clubhouse.

As soon as he was on top of the toy-store roof, Barry began to run. He ran over to the edge of the roof overlooking Main Street, but there was no way down. Barry ran along the roof of the row of old buildings. He suddenly began to realize there might not be a way down.

As he peeked over the front of the shoe store, he saw Josh and John Kramar and some other kids coming up the street.

"Josh, help me!" Barry yelled. The boys down below in the street looked up. They seemed surprised. "Sloan and his club are going to kill me. Get a ladder or something."

Barry looked back. No one had made it up to the roof yet. Down below, Josh and the other boys were talking. They turned and started pedaling down the street away from Barry. As Barry watched them leave, his heart sank.

"Come back!" Barry yelled. He ran along the front of the buildings, but Josh and the others turned the corner and pedaled out of sight.

Barry looked back. He saw a hand grab onto the edge of the roof. Sloan Favor pulled himself up. Barry began to run across the roof tops away from Sloan. He looked back only for an instant. Sloan was helping the others get up on the roof.

Barry ran harder. Soon he would be to the far edge. Deep down, he thought it was no use. That's when he saw the old red bicycle shoot up over the roof. Josh landed the bicycle near an old smokestack.

"How did you . . . I mean . . ." Barry stammered, looking at the odd old bicycle.

"Hop on the back," Josh said simply. Barry hesitated, looking back. Sloan and the other boys were running toward him like a swarm of angry hornets. Barry got on the back of the old red Spirit Flyer. Josh began to pedal straight for the edge of the roof.

"Nooooo!" Barry yelled closing his eyes. He expected to feel the drop any minute. But it never came. All he heard was a whizzing sound. He opened one eye. Instead of hitting the ground, they were higher up in the air. Barry opened both eyes. He was astonished to see several boys and girls on old red Spirit Flyers all around them. He was even more surprised that they were already out of town. Barry looked down. Barry wanted to scream but made a gasping sound instead. They crossed over the Sleepy Eye River which looked no bigger than a ribbon. Barry held on tighter and closed his eyes as the bike zoomed toward the clouds.

THE FARMHOUSE
MEETING

· · · · · · · ·

11

The old red bicycles soared through the air with hardly a sound. Barry hung on with all his might, refusing to open his eyes. "I want to get off," Barry moaned. He wasn't sure what the strange old bike would do next.

"We can't stop now," Josh said over his shoulder. "We have an important meeting to attend. Besides, I think the Three Kings want you at the meeting too."

"The three what?" Barry muttered.

The bicycles flew about eight miles west of town in no time. Josh pointed the handlebars of the old red bicycle toward the ground and glided slowly downward until he was skimming over the tops of the trees. Barry opened one eye. They were dropping down.

The bike glided over a rocky driveway in front of a white farmhouse with blue trim. Beside the farmhouse, there was a long workshop with blue doors and more blue trim. The big blue doors of the workshop opened as the group of bicycle riders got closer. One by one, the bicycles glided through the doors.

"Where are you taking me?" Barry demanded.

"You'll see," Josh said.

The bike glided closer to the ground. Josh and Barry followed Randy through the workshop doors. The big bicycle tires touched down on the cement floor and rolled into a large long room. Tools and benches and boxes were along the walls. A big red tractor was in the center of the room. An old man was sitting on the seat. He looked familiar. Then Barry remembered. He was the old man sitting next to the Kramars at the meeting at the community center.

All the Spirit Flyer bikes rolled up next to the tractor. The riders stayed on. Josh guided his bike right up between the tractor and John Kramar.

"Where are we?" Barry demanded in a whisper. He felt as uneasy around the Spirit Flyer people as he did with Sloan's patrol back in the alley. The other children stared at Barry suspiciously.

"I want to go home," Barry said.

"We'll go home soon enough," Josh said.

"You could at least thank your cousin for saving you," John said.

"Yeah, well . . . I was getting away already," Barry mumbled. "I was about to show those guys up."

"I told you this guy will never change," John said, looking at Barry with disgust.

"Nonsense, my boy," a voice boomed out. The voice belonged to the old man sitting on the tractor. "Everyone can change. Especially once the kings get a good hold on them."

The old man looked right into Barry's eyes as if he knew all about him. Barry felt uneasy though the old man did seem to have a kind face with twinkling eyes.

"Hello, son. My name is John Kramar too," the old man said. "I'm John and Susan's grandfather. And I'm glad you decided to come to our little meeting today."

"But I wasn't trying to come to any meeting," Barry protested. "I was trying to run away from—"

"We all try to run away at one time or another, don't we?" Grandfather Kramar said and winked at Barry. "It's just a good thing the kings can catch us."

Barry felt confused. He looked around the room. He was surprised to see Mrs. Kramar, John's aunt, sitting off to the side on an old Spirit Flyer bicycle too. Some other women from the town were with her. Mrs. Kramar's stomach was very large and bulging since she was going into the last month of her pregnancy. She looked big enough to have a baby any time, Barry thought. He had overheard John say that she was due December 25, Christmas day. She looked at Barry and smiled. All the other children stared at Barry. They didn't seem nearly as friendly as the old man or Mrs. Kramar.

Everyone seemed to be waiting. He stared at the old tractor. Though the tractor looked old and worn, it was still in good shape. And on the red side in noble white letters was the name *Spirit Flyer Harvester*. Barry blinked in surprise. He thought Spirit Flyers were just a brand of bicycles.

"I've been troubled deep inside in my spirit, and I've not been quite sure why," Grandfather Kramar said slowly.

"Because of the war?" John asked.

"The war is part of it, of course," the old man said and sighed. "But I'm more concerned more about the direction our country is headed."

"What do you mean?" Susan Kramar asked.

"I mean that deep inside, war and the fear it brings change people in ways that are hard to imagine," Grandfather Kramar said. "The kings have been showing me something that I think we should all see together. I don't want you to be afraid. I've been asking the Kingson for wisdom and insight because we're going to need it more than ever in the days ahead. That's why I suggested that Bill get this house ready to live in again. I've seen some deeper things regarding the future. I was hoping I was mistaken. But they keep appearing, so I believe the kings are trying to prepare us. So just stay seated on your bikes and watch."

"Do like he says and stay on the bike," Josh commanded. Barry wondered what the old man was talking about. Nothing made much sense to the boy. The old man fiddled with the gears on the tractor and then flipped a switch.

In an instant the room was flooded with a light so bright, it was almost blinding. Barry squinted in surprise and fear. He was about to close his eyes when he saw a brighter light in the midst of the first light. Barry suddenly felt something new and different inside. Though he didn't understand what he was feeling or seeing, he knew he should be quiet and watch. Out of the light, a brilliant shining face appeared.

"The Kingson," Josh whispered. Though he had seen the Kingson several times, Josh never grew tired of looking. The wonder and the excitement was always different.

"Fear not, I am with you, even till the end of this era," the Kingson said in the midst of the light. His voice was strong and filled with power. "Don't be afraid of wars and rumors of evil. This era is passing away, but be at peace, for I am with you always."

The Kingson's face was suddenly gone, though his royal, wonderful presence remained in the room like a sweet fragrance or perfume. Then, in the light before them, a shadow appeared and slowly grew larger, like a cloud forming out of nothing. The black cloud swayed and spun, turning into the shape of a funnel that turned into a miniature tornado swaying and twisting on itself in darkness. That's when below the cloud the picture of a town appeared that looked like one of those tiny towns you see in a model train set.

"Centerville," Josh whispered to Barry.

"I can see that," Barry replied. He looked over at the old red tractor in amazement. The lights of the old machine seemed like a movie projector of some kind. Barry looked back at the scene of the town.

The funnel cloud then touched down on top of the courthouse in the center of town, ripping off the roof. Papers and books and stone blocks and furniture flew off everywhere and were sucked up into the funnel cloud until the inside of the building seemed completely gutted. The only thing left of the courthouse was the outer stone wall.

The churning tornado turned even blacker. Suddenly out of the darkness, two red eyes appeared. Barry's breath caught in his throat. All the children in the room rolled backward on their bikes as they saw the tornado change into a swaying dark snake. Barry felt a surge of fear flash through his body. The large serpent seemed somehow familiar to the boy, as if he'd seen it before, perhaps in a dream.

The gigantic snake rose up over the town as if it owned it. The red eyes flashed and the mouth opened wide. The neck of the snake spread open wide into a hood, like the hood of a cobra. And on the chest of the snake, was a white circle with a white X inside. The snake hissed loudly so that the whole town below trembled and shook. Ancient trees that had stood for over a hundred years in the town square suddenly fell over in a crash.

Silently the snake descended into the gutted shell of the old courthouse. The whole dark body swayed and whirled as it dropped slowly downward. Soon the whole courthouse seemed to be filled with the darkness, as if filled with a pool of hot black tar.

Then in the blink of an eye, on the four stone walls, the sign of the circled X appeared, facing north and south and east and west. The dark clouds of smoke hung over the tiny model city of Centerville.

That's when the people came out. They poured out of the houses all at once, walking and running toward the center of town to the square. Adults and children all seemed to walk automatically to the square, as if drawn by a magnet. Soon the town square was filled with people. Barry was sure he recognized some of the people, like Captain Sharp. Suddenly, a flag was raised on the tall flagpole near the courthouse. The design on the flag was simple: a black cloth with a white circled X in the center. At the sight of the flag, all the people bowed down. Red eyes in the dark windows of the courthouse glowed brightly.

When the bowing people stood up, Barry saw something he hadn't noticed before. All the people had long dark chains wrapped around their bodies, with each chain connected to a big heavy ring around their necks. They all lifted up their right hands, which were each holding a small thin black object about the size of a credit card. Men in gray uniforms came out of the courthouse and walked from person to person, looking at the black objects in the hands of the people.

As suddenly as it began, it was over. The town and people and everything shimmered like a mirage. Then they were gone. The room seemed normal again.

"Remember that the Kingson reminded us not to be afraid," Grandfather Kramar said as the others were rubbing their eyes.

"What does it mean?" Susan Kramar asked. "I got a really bad feeling inside watching that stuff."

"Yeah, what does it mean?" Randy Smedlowe asked.

"The people looked like slaves," John said.

"They were slaves," Mrs. Kramar replied. "I think I know what it means. On one hand I think it means we will lose the election and the courthouse. But I think the courthouse represents something more too. The elections will be for the whole country. I think the law of the land will somehow be affected and taken over by something evil."

"Those gray uniforms are just like the uniforms those ORDER Security Squad people wear," John Kramar said.

Barry was thinking the same thing. He was puzzled. Seeing the scene had made him feel sad and afraid. A great heaviness had seemed to cover him like a suffocating blanket. The feeling would not go away.

"They remind me of the Daimones," Susan Kramar added. She looked at John. He nodded silently.

"What were they holding in their hands?" someone asked.

The other children looked at each other. Then they all spoke at once.

"Number cards," the children said together. The room was very quiet. The impact of what they had just seen was still sinking in.

Barry was confused by it all. He still felt the heaviness. He shuddered. That's when he heard a dull clank. He looked down to see what caused the noise. Barry gasped. A long dark chain was lying on his chest going all the way to the floor where it seemed to just fade into nothingness.

"Aaaackk!" Barry yelped. He quickly grabbed hold of the chain and tried to throw it off of him. But when he jerked it, the chain pulled his neck. Barry panicked. He yanked again and again, but each time he only pulled his head forward. Barry bent over and happened to glance in the broken mirror of Josh's Spirit Flyer. What he saw made him shiver.

The long dark chain was attached securely to a dark metal ring that went all the way around the boy's neck. Barry yanked the chain again and again, harder and harder, but the neck ring only seemed heavier.

"Help!" Barry suddenly yelled. In a panic, he jumped off Josh's bike and ran for the door of the workshop, the long chain clanking as he dragged it with him. He ran outside toward the road. In daylight, he still saw the dark links hanging down his chest. The chain seemed heavier than ever.

Barry ran faster down the gravel driveway. He had almost reached the road when three red Spirit Flyer bikes pulled up ahead of him. John Kramar, Josh and Randy all glided to a halt in front of Barry.

"It's OK," Josh said. "You've discovered the power of your chain."

Barry felt exhausted from running. He stopped and bent over, gasping for air.

"Get it off," Barry cried out. "I want to go home. I hate this place. I want it off me."

"Only the Kingson can unlock your chain," Josh said kindly. "But you have to ask him and bow to him. You're a slave to the chain unless he frees you. But he will free you if you ask him. Then you can belong to him and be in his kingdom."

"Belong to him?" Barry said. "I don't belong to anybody but myself. I just want it off. Make it go away. I don't know what movies you're showing in that workshop or what tricks you're playing, but I don't like them!"

"No trick, no trick," Randy said with a smile. "The kings show you the chain so you can get rid of it."

"Well, I don't want to see any chains," Barry said. "Or snakes or flashy guys made out of light or anything else. I just want to go home."

"But now's a perfect time to get rid of your chain," Josh said. "The Kingson can wipe away all the bad things you've ever said or done, link by link, and make you free."

"I didn't do nothing!" Barry snapped. He suddenly felt defiant. "And I didn't ask to wear any chain."

Though seeing the chain made him feel guilty, Barry didn't understand why. He just wanted the bad feelings to go away. His fear began to turn into anger. He felt hatred swelling up inside him toward whatever or whomever was responsible for causing his bad feelings.

"He won't change," John Kramar grunted. "He's impossible."

"You shut up," Barry said. He spat at John, but the glob of spit sailed by John's head.

Josh looked dismayed. Randy stared at Barry with puzzlement. The dark chain which had been clearly visible began to fade. Barry looked down. He smiled when the chain had totally disappeared.

"See, I didn't need anyone to get rid of it," Barry said in wicked triumph.

"It's still there, whether you see it or not," John Kramar said.

"I told you to shut up," Barry snapped. "You don't know anything!" The group was silent once more.

"Good luck," John said to Josh. "I'll see you guys later." John turned his old red bike and pedaled back toward the workshop.

"I'll take you home," Josh said. "Hop on."

"Just make sure you ride it like a regular bike," Barry insisted.

"We can ride that way, but John Kramar told me it's eight miles back to town from here by the road," Josh said. "Wouldn't you rather fly?"

Barry was silent. In some ways it was thrilling to fly, though he would never admit it to Josh. Somewhere deep inside, flying like that had always been his secret wish. But the Spirit Flyer bikes were too weird. And seeing the chain had upset him.

"Well, I suppose we can fly, but don't go so high," Barry grunted. "I'd be a pile of mush if I fell off."

"Don't worry," Josh said. Barry slowly got on the old bike. Josh began to pedal. As soon as he turned onto the dirt road, he pushed down slowly on the handlebars so they were pointing up. The front wheel of the old bike lifted up into the air, then the rear wheel followed. They were about four feet off the ground when Josh leveled the bike off.

"This ok?" Josh said.

Barry was amazed how smooth the ride felt. Though he felt that vague heaviness around his chest, he couldn't see that mysterious chain. Randy was smiling, flying right alongside of his big brother and Barry.

"This is better," Barry said. Sooner than he thought possible, they touched down on Crofts Road, just outside of Centerville. As they rode into town, Barry hopped off.

"I'm walking the rest of the way," Barry said.

"Why?" Josh asked.

"I have my reasons," Barry grunted. "And it's really none of your business."

"Suit yourself," Josh said. "Come on, Randy."

The two boys rode on ahead. Barry was glad to be alone for a change. He didn't want anyone to see him actually riding on a Spirit Flyer bike. The sun was just beginning to set. By the time he walked up to his driveway, the sky was darkening. The garage door was open. Josh and

Randy were inside looking down at the floor. Barry was about to ignore them when he saw his other bike, or what was left of it, by their feet. The old blue bike had been sawed completely in two. Barry looked at it sadly.

"We just found it out by the side of the house," Josh said. "They must have used a hacksaw. It had this note taped to the handlebars."

Barry looked at the piece of paper. There were only three words scrawled in black ink: *NEXT TIME, SMEDLOWE.*

JOSH'S STORY

· · · · · · · ·

12

Barry put the pieces of the destroyed bicycle in an old shed in the back yard. He trudged upstairs to his room and flopped down in the bed, trying to think. The more he thought, the worse he felt. He took out his number card. As usual, the rank numbers flashed and changed every few seconds. The Point System was still not working. Nothing seemed to be going right, Barry thought.

The last twenty-four hours seemed like a nightmare to the boy. He was in trouble with the police, the whole school thought he was a coward, he had been betrayed by his own friends, his cousins were Rank Blank Spirit Flyer kids, and now his second bike had been destroyed.

He didn't even want to think about the odd movie or whatever it was he had seen coming out of the headlights of that old red tractor. Barry touched his chest, feeling for the chain he had seen. Nothing made sense to the boy. The more he thought, the worse he felt. He wished his whole family could move away to another town somewhere so they could start over, fresh and new.

Barry laid his head on his pillow. He felt tired and closed his eyes. He thought of the dark chain and felt a gnawing fear settle over him like a heavy suffocating blanket. He tossed his head one way and the other, wishing he could sleep. But all he could see was the dark heavy chain hanging down his chest.

"Barry, come eat supper," his father said. Barry opened his eyes. He jumped up. His forehead was damp with sweat.

Barry touched his neck, but the chain wasn't there. He looked in the mirror over his dresser to make sure. Even though he didn't see the chain, Barry still felt a heaviness.

The strange uncomfortable feeling wouldn't leave. Barry shook his head and walked downstairs. The dinner was unusually quiet. At first, Barry thought his father would still be mad about the smoke bomb at the factory. But he seemed distracted instead, as if he were thinking about something else the whole time.

After supper, Mr. Smedlowe called everyone into the living room. He sat down near Josh and Randy. He stared at the older boy.

"I haven't really asked you too much about why you and Randy came to visit us," Mr. Smedlowe said.

"I gave you that package that my dad said to give you," Josh said.

"Yes, I know and I just read the first note, but I was so busy Sunday and Sunday night . . ." Mr. Smedlowe stared at Barry. "As I said, I've been busy. I didn't really get a chance to go over the material your father sent until this afternoon. I probably wouldn't have gone over it then, except Mrs. Smedlowe had read it and seen the tape. She was very concerned."

Barry was surprised at the way his father sounded. His mom looked seriously at Josh and Randy.

"Why don't you tell us what happened before you came here?" Mr. Smedlowe asked.

"Well, I didn't understand all of it," Josh said. "There were a lot of things my dad wouldn't tell us. But as the publisher and editor of the local newspaper, he knew most of what was going on in Hampton. And he wasn't afraid to express his opinions. He wrote most of the editorials in the newspaper himself."

"I've read a number of his editorials over the years," Mr. Smedlowe said. "Your dad and I didn't always see eye to eye, but at least you knew where he stood on issues."

"Well, a lot of the ORDER people didn't like my dad's opinions," Josh said. "They had been around town more than two years, but they didn't really get popular until last winter. A lot of local business people began to support ORDER and their ideas. Many of those businesses were bought up by Goliath Industries. They brought in Big Boards everywhere, into the school system, in all the banks. Everyone was supposed to have number cards. That's when my dad started asking questions and investigating. He wrote an editorial criticizing Big Boards and the Point System and number cards. He made a lot of people mad. Some of the businesses canceled their advertising. Some people wrote mean letters. But a lot of people agreed with my dad too."

Barry listened more closely. Hampton was twice as big as Centerville.

"Things really started to get worse this fall," Josh said. "Like everywhere else, we were scheduled to have elections in early November. In late September, my dad wrote an editorial criticizing the ORDER party platform and local candidates. The way a lot of people reacted, you would have thought he had committed treason. More people canceled their advertising and people canceled subscriptions. We'd get phone calls at all hours of the night with people complaining. The Sheriff, who was an ORDER candidate, started giving my dad parking tickets and stopping him for no reason. They tried to make him change his mind."

"But he only challenged them further, didn't he?" Mrs. Smedlowe asked. "Your dad is an independent thinker, that's for sure."

"He didn't give in at all," Josh said. "But it wasn't just the local people. My dad has a lot of friends who are reporters in the state and elsewhere. A lot of them noticed that ORDER people tried to shut up anyone who disagreed with them. In the middle of October, Sam Waters, a famous magazine reporter and an old friend of my dad's, came to visit in the middle of the night. He said he was in trouble. I'd seen him before. He can be real funny. He knows lots of interesting stories. He's traveled all over the world. Well, he had just come from Europe. He had been writing a story about a new drug called Traginite-Z. Then he wrote about the elections."

"What did you say the name of that drug was?" Mr. Smedlowe asked.

"Traginite-Z," Josh replied. "Sam said it's some new kind of drug that's real unusual. He claims that it's very addictive. Anyway, he was covering that story when his magazine suddenly told him to stop the Traginite-Z story and write about the Euro-central Pact elections. He was surprised, since he was finding out lots of information about this drug and who was selling it. Sam was suspicious, but decided he would go back to the Traginite-Z story after the elections. So, he covered several elections in the Euro-central Pact. ORDER won all the elections, but Sam said they had cheated. Sam had especially investigated the new leader they have there, General Rexoff."

"He's the head of the Euro-central Pact," Mr. Smedlowe said. "He's become very popular in the last month. Everyone says he can bring peace to the whole world."

"That's him," Josh said. "He's on the TV news all the time. Anyway, Sam found out something about this guy that wasn't good, but since Sam's magazine had been recently bought by Goliath Industries, they wouldn't print Sam's story. And not only that, some guys came to Sam's apartment to tell him to leave the country. Sam didn't, he said, because in covering the elections, he had found out some more information about that drug, Traginite-Z and the ORDER political party. He didn't get to follow it through because some more guys came to his hotel, and that time, they tried to hurt him. He escaped again. Sam tried to go to another news magazine with the story, but they wouldn't listen. While he was there, some more ORDER men came and tried to take Sam away. But he got away.

"He had to use a fake passport and everything to fly back to our country. But he wasn't safe here either. He went to his publisher and tried to turn in his story, including his escape from these ORDER guys, only they wouldn't listen. When Sam went back to his hotel room, someone had broken in and stolen all sorts of stuff. But Sam had his story hidden in another place."

"That sounds just like spy stuff in the movies," Barry said. "Are you sure this is true?"

"Go on," Mr. Smedlowe said seriously.

"Well, Sam came to our house next," Josh said. "My dad let him stay in a cabin we own out by a lake. Sam wrote his whole story down and then recorded it on tape. Just before the elections my dad got Sam's permission to run the first part of his story, especially the parts about General Rexoff. My dad hoped other newspapers would print it too. Sometimes they do that. But then the Halloween War happened two days later."

Everyone was silent for a moment. Josh went into the kitchen and returned with a glass of water which he sipped. "After the war, everything changed," Josh said sadly. "Everyone was afraid. We were under emergency law. The ORDER Security Squads were everywhere. A lot of people who had lost their jobs joined the Security Squads. Even though the elections were delayed because of the war, we still had them in our state two weeks later. My dad said people in ORDER took advantage of some loophole or something. He wrote an editorial against having the elections so quickly, especially while we were under martial law. He also started publishing Sam's story again a few days before the elections. But it didn't matter. ORDER won all over the state by a landslide."

"Well, what's wrong with being a winner?" Barry asked.

"There's nothing wrong with winning if you do it fairly," Josh said. "But a lot of strange things started to happen right after the elections. A lot of newspapers shut down. Unless they supported ORDER, no one would support them. My dad said ORDER controlled most of the newspapers and all the radio and TV stations. There were reports that people who had opposed ORDER started to just disappear, but these reports came from friends of my dad. They weren't reported in the news.

"In our town, a man who worked on the election committee came to my dad one night real late. His name was Mr. Sweet. He was upset. He had helped give out the ballots at the election to make sure it was fair. He said that ORDER had a way of marking the ballots so they knew how each person in town voted."

"You mean their votes weren't secret?" Mrs. Smedlowe asked. "How could they do it? I'm on the election board. I'll be there Wednesday to hand out ballots."

"Mr. Sweet said the ballots were numbered secretly, and they would match them up with the person who voted," Josh replied. "I don't know how they did it, but they did. Mr. Sweet saw a secret list he used after the election. He said it showed how each person had voted. And those people who voted against ORDER were marked in red. My dad made a copy of the list and began to watch things. Right away, people on that list left town or disappeared.

"My dad was investigating all this when these men from ORDER came to our house one night. They asked a lot of questions about Sam Waters. My dad wouldn't tell them anything. They got mad and accused him of not being patriotic. They said he was a troublemaker. I think he tried to call you on the telephone around that time, but the phones weren't working. Anyway, they made my dad go down to the Sheriff's office that night. He came back the next morning. That's when he told Randy and me that Sam Waters had been arrested and taken away. Mr. Sweet had also been arrested. My dad gave us that package and told us to be ready to get out of town and come here on a moment's notice. Then, that night after supper, Randy and I were upstairs . . . and we heard the knock on the door . . ."

Josh began to sniffle. He paused and wiped his nose. Randy looked on silently.

"There were all these loud voices and I saw these guys from ORDER," Josh said. "They had guns. They said my mom and dad had to go down to the Sheriff's office for questioning because of Sam Waters and Mr. Sweet. My dad told them Randy and I were over at a friend's house, so they didn't look for us. Anyway, as my dad went to get his coat in the hallway, he could see me up the stairs. He made a motion for me to leave. Then he and my mom left with those guys from ORDER. Randy and I waited until they were gone. Then we took off. We spent the first night at the cabin by the lake. Then we headed here."

No one said a word. Mr. Smedlowe frowned. He stood up and closed the curtains.

"You said that drug he was investigating before the election story was called Traginite-Z?" Mr. Smedlowe asked.

"Yes," Josh said. "Sam was sure it was being produced by Goliath Industries for bad purposes. I'm not sure if it's legal or not. Have you heard of it?"

"As a matter of fact, I have," Mr. Smedlowe said, his face filled with concern. "Our neighbor across the street, Dr. Burke, talked to me a few weeks after the war. He came over one evening, terribly upset. He wanted to talk to someone. He worked at the Goliath factory here in Centerville. He mentioned that drug, Traginite-Z. He claimed that he had examined some candies made by Goliath Industries, called Rainbow Dream Drops. He used his lab at the factory. He said he found traces of Traginite-Z in the candies. He didn't go into great detail, but he said it was an experimental drug with very dangerous properties. He was wondering if I had seen any of that candy at the schools before they closed. He started to tell me something else, but then stopped. He seemed very secretive. He said he would talk to me again the next day."

"What did he say?" Josh asked.

"He didn't come back," Mr. Smedlowe replied. "Dr. Burke was sent to Europe the next day to work on a special assignment. At least that's what Mrs. Burke says. I went over to talk to her a few days later since he didn't show up. She didn't know anything about Traginite-Z. She also wasn't sure when her husband would be home. She's been quite concerned because she's all alone with her baby and Amy, her stepdaughter. She thought he would return after three weeks, but a Goliath company official came by and told her that he was involved in a top-secret project and would be gone at least another month. She said they are paying her well, but she's still upset. I hadn't heard or read anything else about Traginite-Z until you just mentioned it. I wonder what's really going on."

"Well, if it involves ORDER or Goliath, who knows?" Josh said. "I think we're all in for a lot of trouble if they win the elections."

Everyone was quiet. Outside, the wind began to blow and rain started to fall.

ELECTION
DAY
· · · · · · · · ·
13

Election day came with a storm. The sky was overcast and dark. Barry didn't sleep well after hearing Josh's story. He woke up three times in the night from bad dreams. When he got up, he felt terrible, not only from lack of sleep but from a great heaviness he felt inside. He was desperately afraid of his old friends and the ridicule of Sloan Favor and the other Super Wings. The more he thought about it, the more convinced he was that they would try to hurt him again. His stomach twisted in pain.

Barry got out of bed and went into the hall. He was heading downstairs, when he heard his parents whispering. Their door was opened a crack and Barry put his ear closer.

"I think you have to do something," Mrs. Smedlowe said urgently. "You have influence. You're the school principal."

"We went through this all last night," Mr. Smedlowe said irritably. "I can't just stop supporting ORDER. I would lose my job in two seconds if I spoke out against them."

"Your brother wasn't afraid to speak up," Mrs. Smedlowe said. "He did the right thing."

"And look what happened to him," Mr. Smedlowe replied.

"That's what I mean," Mrs. Smedlowe whispered angrily. "Do you want that kind of thing going on around here?"

"Of course not," Mr. Smedlowe said. "But I'm just one man. And besides, we don't know the full story in this situation. My brother has often been a champion for lost causes, and sometimes foolish causes, in my opinion. Maybe his facts were messed up."

"Then why did he send his own children away to protect them from danger? And why can't you reach him by phone? You read those papers and have that reporter's book and tapes. Don't you believe what he said about that awful General Rexoff?"

Barry's eyes went wide. His parents hadn't mentioned having those things last night. And Josh had never said anything about it.

"It's too late in the game to suddenly switch teams," Mr. Smedlowe said. "We can't afford to be unemployed. Maybe it was just an isolated incident back in Hampton. Maybe once the new government gets rolling, things will get better. That's all ORDER wants. They want to bring peace."

"But what kind of peace is it if people can't write an editorial in a newspaper without being afraid the police will come haul them off in the night?" Mrs. Smedlowe demanded. There was a long pause inside the room. Barry leaned closer to the door. "Who would have ever thought our country could come to this? I can't believe things have changed so much in such a short time."

"Who would have thought the government would be in such a shambles?" his father replied. "Who would have thought there would be war again? War brings changes. All I know is that by tonight, ORDER will most likely be in power in this town, state and nation. They seem to have the best plans going for recovery. I think we should just wait this thing out, not make a fuss, and see what happens."

Barry backed away from the door. When his father came out into the hall, he looked worried and angry. His eyes looked especially tired.

The breakfast table was tense that morning. Mr. Smedlowe ate busily. Barry could tell his father just wanted to get out of the house. His mother seemed angry. She sloshed his dad's coffee when she poured him a second cup. Josh and Randy ate cereal quietly.

"Mrs. Smedlowe and I will be down at the school most of the day today," Mr. Smedlowe said to Josh and Randy. "I hope you boys understand. We've been committed to helping out in this election for some time. It would look awfully strange if I tried to back out on election day. I've committed myself to certain work, and I have to keep my commitments."

"I understand," Josh said simply. "It doesn't really matter. We know ORDER will win, at least in the elections today. We've all seen it. Even Barry saw it, right?"

"What do you mean you 'saw it'?" Mrs. Smedlowe asked. "What did you see, Barry?"

"I don't know what he's talking about," Barry lied. "I've got to go." He got up and went upstairs. After hesitating for a few seconds, he got out his gray ORDER uniform and put it on. He looked sadly at the Cobra patch on the shoulder. He thought about his old friends.

"They'll come back to my side," Barry muttered to himself. "Once they get tired of that dictator Sloan, they'll come back, and we'll have the biggest and best patrol of all the ORDER commandos."

Barry walked briskly downstairs. Josh was in the living room and looked up. He frowned when he saw Barry's uniform.

"Are you still going to hang out with those guys?" Josh asked. "Didn't you even hear what I said last night?"

"I heard you," Barry said simply. "But you've got to face facts. After all, you said ORDER would win. And I want to stick with the winners. They can't be so bad, or why would so many people support them?"

"Because people are afraid to stand up for what's right if it means being unpopular," Josh replied. "That's what my dad always said. And he was right."

"Well, my dad says we should just wait the election out and see what happens," Barry said. "He doesn't think ORDER is so terrible."

"I think you'll regret the day you ever saw one of those gray uniforms," Josh said.

Barry grunted. He got an umbrella from the closet and walked outside into the stormy December day. He walked down Buckingham and over to Main Street, heading for the square. The Centerville streets were bustling that day. Seeing them reminded Barry of old times, the way Centerville used to be.

Political signs were planted in lawns everywhere. Almost all of them said *VOTE ORDER.* There were some other signs in people's yards, but they had either been marked on or ripped up. Barry saw one man, Mr. Fenster, frowning as he picked up the pieces of a destroyed sign.

"What's eating that old goat?" Barry said to himself.

Security Squad vehicles cruised the streets. Some were escorting people to the voting polls over at the school, others just seemed to be driving slowly around, patrolling the streets.

Barry walked to the town square, turned east and walked toward the school. When he got closer, he was surprised to see a huge group of children wearing their ORDER uniforms at the far end of the parking lot.

Barry ran over. They were in some sort of meeting, but just as Barry got there, the meeting broke up. Sloan Favor, Jason and other kids in the Super Wings Patrol were talking to Captain Sharp. Barry stepped behind Captain Sharp's jeep. After talking a few minutes, the Super Wings kids left on their bicycles. They each carried packets of what looked like brochures. Barry waited until everyone he knew was gone. Then he walked slowly over to Captain Sharp.

"I didn't know there was a meeting this morning," Barry said. "What's going on? Are they all helping with the election today? I'd like to help too."

"They are helping," Captain Sharp said, packing things into a black briefcase. He seemed busy and annoyed. Then he looked up at Barry. "Those children, unlike yourself, are not on suspended status from ORDER activities. They have proven themselves capable of carrying out orders without messing up. There is also no question about their loyalties."

"I'm loyal," Barry said.

"I heard some disturbing reports about you yesterday," Captain Sharp said. He stared at Barry. "It seems you were seen keeping company with known Rank Blank children. Sloan Favor and several of your friends reported the same story."

"I couldn't help it," Barry protested. "Sloan was out to kill me. I was trying to run away and Josh helped me out."

"So you were riding with them?" Captain Sharp said. "Sloan said he and the other boys were playing a practical joke. Where did you go and what did you do with them?"

"I just got away, that's all," Barry lied.

"The way I understood it, you provoked Sloan and the others," Captain Sharp said. "All the boys said they were trying to work together and you tried to steal their clubhouse. Then they said you ran off, taking up with those Rank Blank children, known enemies of ORDER. I must say, I'm beginning to wonder about you, young man. I thought you were solidly on the side of ORDER."

"But I am on the side of ORDER," Barry said.

"It's out of my hands," Captain Sharp said simply, snapping his briefcase shut. "I wish I could include you in today's election activities and invite you to tonight's victory celebration, but there are too many problems. And until this matter with the police is settled, it's best if you are not seen as being associated with ORDER. We don't want the community to get the idea that we are involved with the kind of behavior you displayed this last Sunday night."

"But all that was your idea!" Barry protested. "I wouldn't have even been there unless you had given us that smoke bomb."

Captain Sharp looked suddenly into Barry's eyes. The Captain's eyes seemed to pierce right through him. "Shifting the blame on others won't help you out," Captain Sharp said. "I thought I warned you about that already."

"Yes, but . . ."

The Captain kept staring. Barry didn't say a word. He felt extremely uncomfortable.

"I think it's better that you go home and take off that uniform, until your suspension is lifted," Captain Sharp said. "Now I must be about my business."

Captain Sharp got in his black jeep and drove off. Barry stood in the parking lot all alone. He felt the familiar heavy feeling descend on him all over again. He muttered as he walked across the parking lot. The big gymnasium doors were open. People were walking inside to vote. Barry went over to take a better look. He knew his parents had to be inside somewhere.

The gymnasium smelled like it always did, of wood and old tennis shoes. There were tables and little booths with curtains all arranged in a row. People were in line in front of a long table. Barry's mother and another woman, Mrs. Gilmore, were checking lists of names. His mom seemed busy, but she did smile when she saw Barry. After Mrs. Gilmore checked to see if a person was eligible to vote, she stamped their voter registration card. They showed Barry's mother the stamped card. She had them sign a sheet of paper on a clipboard. She then pulled a ballot out of a box and gave it to the person. They carried the ballot to one of the curtained booths. When they were finished voting, they dropped the ballots into a large metal box that was closed with a padlock.

Mr. Smedlowe came into the room with two men and a woman, school-board members. Mr. Smedlowe seemed busy. When he saw Barry, he walked over.

"You shouldn't be here," Mr. Smedlowe said. "Why don't you go play with your friends?"

"I was just looking," Barry said glumly. He didn't feel like explaining that he wasn't sure he even had any friends. Barry watched the people dropping ballots into the metal box. "Do you think ORDER is cheating somehow?"

"Barry!" his father whispered. "Don't even say that. I don't want you mentioning Josh's story to anyone, do you understand?"

"Do you believe what Josh said?" Barry asked.

"Don't be so loud," Mr. Smedlowe whispered. "I'm not sure what I believe," Mr. Smedlowe whispered. "But this isn't the time or place to discuss it. Now run along."

His father sounded just like he always sounded when he was acting as the principal. Barry didn't say anything, but walked out the door.

After school, the walk home seemed especially lonely. There were children in the gray ORDER uniforms, busily going from house to house on every street. Barry felt left out. He even hid behind trees two different times to avoid meeting kids in the Super Wings Patrol. When he got home, he was glad that Josh and Randy were gone. Rain began to fall from the dark sky just as he shut the front door.

The day dragged by. Barry stayed in the house. His father came home for a quick supper and left again. Josh and Randy came in soon after, but they went back out too. Around seven o'clock both Barry's parents came home. Right away Barry could tell that something was wrong. His mother was near tears.

"I won't take it back," Mrs. Smedlowe said, her voice cracking. "It's not like they need that list. It's not official. We never had a list like that when we voted before."

"That's not the point," his dad said, loosening his tie. He slumped down into a chair. "I think you could get into a lot of trouble if they found out."

"I don't care. I'll just say the list got lost," Mrs. Smedlowe replied. "It's just like Josh said. I think they marked the ballots somehow. The election people were awfully particular that I not give the ballots out of order. They had to come right off the top as each person signed in."

"I didn't see any numbers or suspicious marks on the ballots when I voted," Mr. Smedlowe said. "What did you do with the list?"

"I have it in my purse, and I will put it in a safe place," she said. She wiped her eyes and walked quickly upstairs.

"What's going on?" Barry asked.

"Oh, Barry, I didn't see you," Mr. Smedlowe said.

"Mom looked like she was crying," Barry said.

"She's just had a hard day," his father replied. "Don't worry. We've got to go out to a victory party at the country club. Everyone will be celebrating as the votes come in."

Mr. Smedlowe went upstairs. Barry followed him. He tried to listen at their bedroom door, but it was shut tight. He could tell they were arguing, but he couldn't understand the words.

His parents went out to the Goliath Country Club a half-hour later. Josh and Randy came home just as they were leaving. Mrs. Smedlowe spoke quietly with Josh for a few minutes. Barry tried to eavesdrop but couldn't hear a word.

After his parents went to the club, Barry, Josh and Randy watched the TV. The only thing that was on was news about the elections. All over the country and even in other countries around the world, ORDER candidates were reported as winning their elections. Barry hardly spoke to the other boys. Randy asked Josh questions and Josh tried to explain what was happening.

By nine o'clock, people from ORDER were declaring victory in almost all of the elections. Barry felt bored and tired of all the speeches. People kept saying the same things—a new age of peace and safety was beginning, and people didn't need to be afraid of war. All the people were making the ORDER salute, crossing their arms across their chests. "Just like they said, ORDER wins," Barry announced to the other boys. Josh and Randy were quiet. "I'm going up to my room."

Barry lay down on his bed to read. He was tired. He closed his eyes after reading a few pages in the ORDER Patrol book. A noise woke him. He looked up. The clock said it was past midnight. He heard noises in the hall. He was alarmed until he heard his parents' voices. They sounded upset. Barry turned off his bedroom light and opened his door a crack to listen better.

"I told you they would ask questions," his father said angrily. "Captain Sharp was very annoyed that the list was missing. When he finds it's not in that box of election materials, he'll ask more questions. You can count on it."

"That just proves my point," his mother said. "Why would he be so interested in that list if it doesn't mean anything? Josh's story was true. They want it to know who voted against them."

"That doesn't prove anything of the kind," Mr. Smedlowe said. "This was an official election. Naturally they want their paperwork to be in order. These are government bureaucrats. If they have their papers out of order they're in trouble, just like I would be if I had sloppy paperwork."

"I don't believe it and neither do you," his mom said. "I'd better check on Barry."

Barry dove for the bed. He had just pulled up the covers when his mother opened the door. She stood there silently for a moment and then closed the door. Barry scurried out of bed to listen again, but his parents had apparently stopped speaking to each other.

TRAITOR

· · · · · · · ·

14

As Barry walked to school the next morning, he heard a noise moving slowly behind him. He turned as Captain Sharp's black jeep pulled up to the curb. The window went down.

"Peace and safety," the Captain said, making the ORDER salute.

"Yeah, peace and safety," Barry said without much enthusiasm.

"You don't sound as happy as a good citizen should after ORDER's glorious victory in yesterday's elections," the Captain said.

"Why should I be happy?" Barry grunted. "Nobody included me in the party."

"That was because you had been careless last Sunday night," Captain

Sharp said. "Sheriff Burns, our new man, should be able to help you in your case, assuming, of course, you can prove you're loyal to ORDER. As I said, you were careless, and that concerns us, especially since carelessness seems to run in your family."

"What do you mean?" Barry asked.

"It seems a valuable list was lost yesterday," Captain Sharp. "And your mother was in charge of that list. Now that list seems to have disappeared."

"What does that have to do with me?" Barry asked. "I didn't lose it."

"Well, it just strikes us as odd that we have two incidents of carelessness so close together with two members of the same family involved," Captain Sharp said. "It's even more suspicious that these incidents occurred just when two other family members began living in your home, and these family members happen to be vocal opponents of ORDER."

"I can't help it if my cousins don't like ORDER!" Barry exclaimed.

"Perhaps it is just a coincidence," Captain Sharp said. "But we noticed last night that your mother seemed to be upset and worried. Has she been that way around the house?"

Captain Sharp leaned forward and stared carefully into Barry's eyes. Barry looked down.

"You haven't seen some sheets of blue paper with names listed on them, have you?" Captain Sharp asked. "She may have left them on a table or a desk?"

"I haven't seen a thing," Barry said. "I can't help it if she made some mistake."

"It would be very much to your advantage if you helped us correct this mistake," Captain Sharp replied. His eyes seemed like needles looking into Barry. "Now why don't you tell me what you heard your mother say about that list?"

Barry paused. He was surprised Captain Sharp was so concerned. Maybe the list was important, like his mother thought.

"I don't know anything. I told you," Barry said.

"There will probably be a reward for the recovery of that list, if it has been lost."

"A reward?" Barry asked. "What kind of reward?"

"It is a very valuable list," the Captain said. "The reward would be a top-of-the-line Super Wings bicycle, loaded with extras. We could fix you up with a bicycle even better than Sloan Favor's bike."

"Really?" Barry asked. He licked his lips.

"You think about it," Captain Sharp said dryly, "as you walk to school. Sometimes walking can improve a boy's memory."

The Captain drove off. The officer from ORDER drove directly to the Centerville school. He parked by the bicycle racks. Sloan Favor and several other boys were talking as they locked up their bikes. They ran over to see Captain Sharp. After talking to them a few moments, the captain drove off. As he drove, he picked up the red radio microphone.

"I didn't learn anything from the Smedlowe boy," Captain Sharp said. "But he seems to know more than he's saying. I think he just needs a little more softening up before he can decide to do the right thing. I'll be using the Favor boy to help out. He's eager. Before long, I'm sure the Smedlowe boy will confess everything he knows."

Barry got to school just as the bell was ringing. He was surprised to see more than two-thirds of his class wearing their gray ORDER uniforms to school. Barry wished he had worn his uniform too. He slumped down in his seat and tried to avoid looking at any of his old friends. Josh was sitting next to John Kramar and the other group of kids who had Spirit Flyers. Barry felt like he didn't fit in anywhere.

On his way to gym class, he decided it might be better to be a little late. He wanted to avoid meeting up with Sloan. Barry went into the boy's bathroom in the hall near the gym. The bathroom was empty. Barry looked at himself in the mirror. He was combing his hair when the door flung open. Barry flinched. Jason and Roger walked in.

"Look who's here!" Jason said. They were carrying gym bags. The bathroom door banged open again. Sloan Favor and several other seventh graders swaggered in. Each one was carrying his gym bag. Barry took a few steps back. Sloan didn't say a word. He unzipped his gym bag. He looked at the other boys. They unzipped their gym bags too. Without speaking, Sloan reached in his bag and took out two small white objects. Barry realized they were eggs just as Sloan cocked back his arm to throw them. Barry tried to duck, but the eggs hit him right on the head. A terrible smell filled his nostrils. The eggs were rotten. Two more crashed into him as he tried to run for a bathroom stall, but he slipped on egg goo and fell to the floor. He was immediately pelted by a barrage of splattering rotten eggs which popped as they hit him. Barry covered his head with his hands, but it was no protection. In seconds, he was covered with sickly yellowish-gray egg yolks. Bits of egg shell were everywhere. The awful smell was suffocating.

"This is what happens to chickens who run away," Sloan Favor announced. "This is also what happens to rotten eggs like you, traitors against ORDER. Do you hear me?"

Barry didn't say a word. Sloan walked over to Barry. Without warning, he kicked Barry right in the ribs. Barry yelped as the blow knocked him over. His ribs felt like they were on fire. Sloan walked away.

"Hey, Barry, you better clean up," Jason said. Barry looked up. Jason threw a roll of toilet paper which bounced off Barry's head and landed in the slimy egg goo on the floor. The boys giggled as they quickly left the room. Barry slipped twice as he struggled to his feet.

Barry limped out of the bathroom and went outside. When his father saw him in the hallway, he didn't even ask what happened. He just told Barry in a disgusted tone of voice to go home and get cleaned up. The awful smell stayed with him as he headed for home. He was two blocks away from Buckingham Street when a black jeep with a flashing red light on top pulled in front of him. Barry stopped as Captain Sharp got out. He smiled when he saw Barry. "Peace and safety," the Captain said. "I just got a report about your little incident in the bathroom. It's a shame

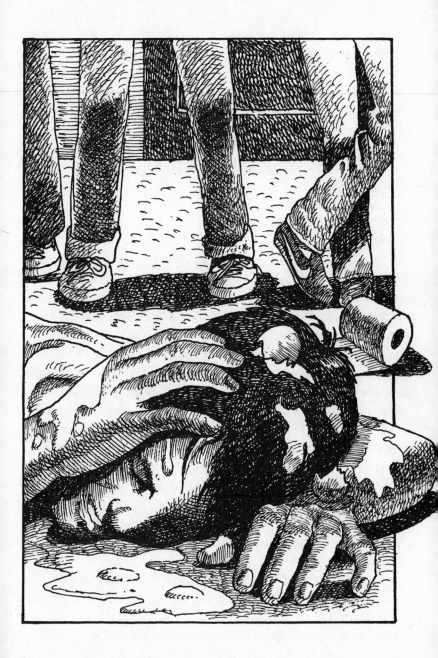

what some boys will do to another boy whom they suspect of being a traitor."

"But I'm no traitor," Barry protested. "I've tried to do everything you asked."

"I've heard all your excuses," the Captain said. "The sooner you learn excuses and lies don't work, the better. You can fool your friends and parents and teachers, but you can't fool the Big Board or the people in ORDER for very long. You're just like your mother. We know she's not telling the truth either."

"You do?" Barry asked. "If that's so, why do you want me to tattle on her?"

"We don't want you to be a tattletale. This isn't a game at recess, boy. We want you to be loyal to your government. Your mother has broken the law."

"So why don't you arrest her or something?" Barry asked. "Why do you keep bothering me?"

"Because we need . . . a witness, not a tattletale, to give her name, as a legal precaution," the Captain said. "We also want to give you a chance to save yourself. I'm afraid today's incident in the bathroom is only the beginning. All loyal ORDER Commandos could soon make you the target of all kinds of pranks if they think you are a traitor. You wouldn't want that, would you?"

The Captain paused, smiling. Barry knew that a lot of kids had grudges against him from the past. Even without ORDER, many kids would have lots of reasons to get back at him. Thinking of those possibilities made the boy feel desperate and scared. Yet the Captain was asking him to be a tattletale on his own mother. Barry felt tears of frustration beginning to creep into his eyes.

"If you know about a crime against the state and you refuse to cooperate and tell the authorities about it, you are considered a partner in that crime," the Captain said seriously. "You could be in as much trouble as your mother will be if she continues to defy us."

"But what do I have to do?" Barry asked weakly.

"Prove your loyalty," the Captain quickly said. "Be a witness and tell the truth about what your mother did."

"What kind of loyalty is that?" Barry asked. He felt confused and afraid.

"It's for her own good," Captain Sharp said. "Do you want her to go to jail?"

"You said if I knew about a crime, I would be a partner, but if I knew about something else, would that count? I mean, I'm not sure, but I think I know someone who is in trouble with ORDER for sure. And I can prove it."

"What are you talking about?"

"Well, I told you I have these Rank Blank cousins," Barry said. "But you don't know the whole story of how they came here or about their father. Josh and Randy had to leave in the middle of the night because his parents did something against the government where they used to live. So they are lawbreakers too. If I told you some stuff about them, wouldn't that be enough? That would show I'm loyal, and then you could tell all my friends and they would be nice to me again."

"This sounds interesting. Tell me more," Captain Sharp said.

Barry began to tell the story about Josh and Randy. Captain Sharp taped every word Barry said. As soon as he mentioned General Rexoff and the reporter's name, Barry could tell the Captain was very interested. And the more he talked, the more interested Captain Sharp looked.

When he was finished, Captain Sharp was smiling. Barry was sure he had forgotten all about his mother and the election list.

"We'll deal with this as soon as the paperwork is complete," the Captain said. "I'll be by your house within an hour with some papers for you to sign." The black jeep sped quickly down the street. Barry felt sick to his stomach. The stench of rotten eggs filled his nose and mouth.

Barry was fidgeting that evening. All he could think about was the papers that he had signed that morning. Captain Sharp had been so impatient that Barry didn't even read the report. He just signed his name.

"I did the right thing," Barry muttered to himself. "It will help Mom and Dad."

Avoiding his cousins that evening wasn't easy, but Barry did his best. He ate his supper in silence. Barry could tell that his parents were still upset. Right after supper, there was a loud knocking at the door.

"Who could that be?" Mr. Smedlowe asked. He was surprised to see Captain Sharp.

"Captain Sharp, what brings you out tonight?" Mr. Smedlowe asked. "Come inside."

The Captain came in with four other men in gray ORDER uniforms. They frowned at Mr. Smedlowe. Josh and Randy came down the stairs to see who was at the door. Mrs. Smedlowe came out of the kitchen. Barry thought she flinched when she saw the men from ORDER.

"Is there some problem?" Barry's father asked.

"Yes, I'm afraid there is a problem," Captain Sharp said. "It's come to our attention that you have fugitives from the Hampton police living here. You are also acting as guardians without legal approval of the government."

"What are you talking about?" Mr. Smedlowe asked.

"We have orders to take into custody one Joshua Smedlowe, age twelve, and one Randolph Smedlowe, age ten. Do you deny they are living here?"

"No, but what have they done?" Mr. Smedlowe asked. "What right do you have to take them?"

"They are suspected of criminal activities. But we have a right to take them because they are legally wards of the state. Their parents are under arrest, and you are not their legal guardians."

"But I am their legal guardian," Mr. Smedlowe said.

"Can you prove that?" Captain Sharp asked in a stony voice.

"Well, there's a will somewhere and. . . ."

The men from ORDER moved over to Josh and Randy. They weren't even listening to Mr. Smedlowe's explanation.

"Hold on, just a minute," Mr. Smedlowe said loudly when he saw that the men were serious. "I demand an explanation."

"A complaint was signed against these boys," Captain Sharp said. He held up a piece of official-looking paper. "We have testimony that they participated in illegal activities, transporting and keeping stolen state documents."

"Who told you this ?" Mr. Smedlowe asked. "Who signed it?"

"One Barry S. Smedlowe," Captain Sharp said impatiently.

"Barry?" Mr. Smedlowe turned and looked at his son.

"I did it to help them, Dad," Barry said. "They're criminals. All that will happen is that they'll go to a school somewhere. Besides, we'd all get in trouble keeping them here. We'd be helping criminals, and we could get in trouble for that."

Josh stared at Barry in disbelief. "You turned us in?" he asked. Barry had never had anyone look at him the way Josh did at that moment.

"Here's the order, signed by the judge." Captain Sharp handed Mr. Smedlowe the documents.

Mr. and Mrs. Smedlowe crowded together to read the papers. Mrs. Smedlowe put her hand over her mouth. Barry was surprised when she started to cry.

"I don't wanna go. I don't wanna go," Randy screeched. The little boy started to run, but he was caught in the large arms of the uniformed men. They laughed and pulled his skinny arms behind his back.

"Don't hurt him, you bullies," Josh yelled. He lunged for the men holding his brother. Captain Sharp stepped in his way and pulled Josh's arm. But Josh yanked away. Captain Sharp reached again and Josh twirled around, his fist flying. He hit Captain Sharp squarely in the nose. The Captain fell backward and tripped. On the floor, he looked totally surprised. Then he was full of rage.

"Get that brat!" the Captain hissed.

The two other guards were on Josh in an instant. Randy was still screaming. Barry had backed against the wall. He had never seen a boy hit an adult. Captain Sharp's face was churning with anger.

Barry's mother cried louder as they pulled the two children out the front door. Captain Sharp wiped a trickle of blood off his lip with a handkerchief.

"If you have any questions, we'll be at the Sheriff's office," Captain Sharp said. He turned and followed his men to the jeeps.

"Don't let them do it, Robert!" Mrs. Smedlowe said to her husband. "Can't you stop them?"

"He has papers," he said. "We can't disobey a court order."

While they were talking, the black jeeps sped away into the night. The men from ORDER were gone almost as quickly as they had come. The air was thick with violence and fear. Barry felt sick inside. He kept seeing Josh's stare.

"Barry, how could you?" Mrs. Smedlowe cried out. "How could you do that to your own flesh and blood?"

"I did it to help all of us, Mommy," Barry said. "Captain Sharp wanted me to turn you in. He knows you took that list, Mommy. He was asking me all about it. He wanted me to sign a paper against you. I didn't know what to do. I knew you took it. I heard you talking last night. They would have come for you, but I gave them Josh and Randy. I had to do it. And I say good riddance. They would have gotten us all in trouble. I want to be on the side of the winners for a change."

Both parents looked surprised. Mr. Smedlowe sat down heavily on a chair.

"I told you not to cooperate with those people," Mrs. Smedlowe said to her husband, and she began to sob again.

"And I told you not to take that list," Mr. Smedlowe whispered angrily. Soon both his parents were arguing. Barry ran upstairs to his room. The plan wasn't turning out at all like he expected. He thought his parents would be pleased that he helped them, especially his mother. But she looked at him like he was a traitor. Barry felt confused, guilty and upset.

A few minutes later, his father appeared at his door, his face serious. He cleared his throat.

"Get on your coat," Mr. Smedlowe said. "We're going down to the Sheriff's office and see if we can straighten this mess out."

"Do I have to?" Barry asked. He dreaded the thought of seeing Josh again.

"Yes. Don't argue." Mr. Smedlowe waited as Barry slowly got his coat from the closet.

The whole Smedlowe family arrived down at the Sheriff's office that evening just past eight o'clock. Barry was surprised to see John and Susan Kramar there. They were carrying boxes to a car by the curb. Sheriff Kramar wasn't wearing his uniform. Barry realized he wasn't sheriff anymore.

"Evening, Bill," Mr. Smedlowe said to Mr. Kramar.

"I heard about your nephews," Mr. Kramar said. He looked at Barry for a moment. "I'd help you out on this, but I'm no longer sheriff as of five o'clock tonight. They got those papers from the judge without my help."

"We'll straighten this out soon enough," Mr. Smedlowe said confidently. "I've got Peek and Penn, Attorneys-at-Law, on the case. They are meeting us here. I never thought I'd be in a spot like this."

"You may be in for a real surprise before this is all over," Mr. Kramar said glumly. "You haven't dealt with these people like I have. They're tough."

Another car drove up. Two middle-aged men got out. Barry had seen them before, but he wasn't sure of their names.

"Who are they?" Barry asked.

"That's Peek and Penn," Barry's dad said. "They'll help us get Josh and Randy back. I hope."

The two men both wore red suspenders and glasses. They looked a bit annoyed at being called out so suddenly in the night. Their suit coats were rumpled. Penn was tall and thin. Peek was short and heavyset. Both men appeared to be a little older than Mr. Smedlowe. The Smedlowes and the attorneys walked into the Sheriff's office.

Barry sat on a green wooden bench by the sidewalk. John and Susan Kramar looked at him silently.

"You really fixed it for your cousins," John said, shaking his head.

"Of all the rotten things you've ever done, how could you turn your own family over to those men, Barry?" Susan asked. Her eyes flashed with anger.

"You guys don't know anything," Barry snapped. "Leave me alone."

Mr. Kramar walked down the sidewalk. He looked back at the Sheriff's office wistfully. They got in the car and then drove away.

If there was anything Barry hated, it was waiting. When it seemed like his parents and the two lawyers had been inside for hours, they came down the sidewalk. Mr. Smedlowe was frowning. His mother looked like she had been crying, but had no tears left. She seemed very tired.

"They have Josh and Randy at the Security Squad Center out on Cemetery Road, and they will not release them," Mr. Smedlowe said. He started the car and drove home. No one said a word.

Barry went straight to bed, but he couldn't sleep. Every time he closed his eyes, he kept seeing the look of betrayal and surprise on Josh's face.

"I did it for our good," Barry repeated to himself softly. But no matter how many times he said it, he couldn't convince himself.

BARRY ON
THE SCALES
· · · · · · · · ·
15

Barry had always secretly thought people didn't like him, but he had always hoped that it really wasn't true. As he woke up that next morning, he realized his secret hopes were pure daydreams. He knew no one liked him. His old friends, the other kids at school and even his parents seemed disgusted with him. And as Barry thought about it, he realized that he didn't really want to be with himself either. He secretly wished he were dead.

"I might as well be dead, the way people are treating me," he muttered bitterly. "No one cares about me. They all hate me and think I'm rotten. And they're probably right."

Barry pulled his New Improved Number Card out of his pocket. The scores flashed on and off, on and off, nonsense numbers. The boy sighed and put the card back in his pocket.

Barry didn't eat breakfast. He waited upstairs, slowly getting dressed, only coming downstairs when it was time to go to school. His father had already left and his mother looked very tired and worn. Dark splotches were under her eyes. She looked at Barry but didn't say anything. Her silence said more than the boy could bear. Barry took a deep breath and went outside.

He trudged to school, his steps heavy on the sidewalk. Other children rode by on bikes, but Barry kept his eyes on the ground. He didn't want to speak to anyone or have them speak to him. He was afraid of what they would say. Fear gripped his stomach so badly that Barry stopped several times, feeling that he needed to catch his breath. Barry had a headache all that morning in school. The Spirit Flyer kids ignored him in stony silence. Everyone knew that Josh and Randy had been taken by the police, turned in by Barry. Barry had secretly hoped that turning in Josh would make Sloan and the other kids look on him more favorably. But when Barry tried to sit next to Jason, Alvin and Roger at lunchtime, they all held their noses.

"Something smells rotten," Jason said.

"Yeah, like rotten eggs," Roger agreed. The boys broke out laughing. Barry moved away and ate lunch alone.

The school day seemed to take forever. After the final bell, Barry walked slowly toward home, watching the streets carefully so he wouldn't have to face any of his classmates. A horn honked behind him. Barry was surprised to see Captain Sharp parked by the curb. The Captain waved for Barry to come over. Barry was even more surprised.

"Peace and safety," the Captain said as Barry walked over.

"Peace and safety," Barry said, even though he didn't feel peaceful or at all safe.

"I have good news for you, my boy," the Captain said.

"Really?" Barry asked.

"The new sheriff and some others in power are looking on you with favor, lucky for you," Captain Sharp said. "They are beginning to believe that you really are one of us."

"Oh?" Barry asked. Barry was surprised that the Captain seemed to be in such a good mood.

"They are trusting you with another mission," Captain Sharp said. "If you pass this test, you can prove yourself worthy. You'll be high up in the point system and high up in the ranks of ORDER."

"What do I have to do?" Barry asked suspiciously.

"We've heard that those Rank Blank Spirit Flyer people are getting together this afternoon," Captain Sharp said.

"Why don't you go and stop it then?" Barry asked.

"Well, we don't want to stop it," Captain Sharp said. "All we want is for you to take a picture of them meeting with one of our new surveillance cameras."

"What kind of camera?" Barry asked.

"It's called a Nega-Cam," the Captain said. He lifted a black object from the seat. Though it looked something like a small video camera, it was unlike anything Barry had ever seen before. A large white circled X was printed on both sides. Below the circle were the words *Goliath Nega-Cam*.

"How does it work?" Barry asked.

"It's too technical for me to explain," Captain Sharp said. "It's one of Goliath's new experimental cameras using digital disks. They say it can see deeper and more intensely than any other camera ever made. Once someone shoots . . . I mean, takes a picture with this camera, it reveals much more than an ordinary tape or photo."

"And all I have to do is take pictures of them meeting?" Barry asked. "Why do you need me?"

"Well, as I said, the Nega-Cam is a special experimental device," the Captain replied. "And we need a traitorous human . . . I mean, a boy like you, about your age, to try it out for us. Actually, it's a great privilege for you. I assured my superiors that you'd jump at the chance. After all, there is a reward if you shoot the Nega-Cam just right . . . and it will further prove your loyalty and desire to work with ORDER."

"I don't know," Barry said. He stared at the Nega-Cam suspiciously. Something about the black camera made him feel uneasy. "Where are they meeting?"

"They're meeting out at a farm outside of town. The Kramars own this farm. I will drive you, at least most of the way. You can then pedal your new bicycle to take the pictures and then meet me at the road again."

"What new bicycle?" Barry said glumly.

"The brand new Goliath Super Wings I have in the back of my jeep," Captain Sharp said with a tight smile. "And once you complete your mission, the new bike will be yours to keep. Perhaps we can even forget about your mother's problem."

"Really?" Barry asked eagerly. That was the best news he'd heard all day. But then he paused. "Are you sure this isn't some kind of bomb?"

"It's just a special camera, that's all," Captain Sharp said impatiently. He put the Nega-Cam back down in the seat. "As I said, it would be difficult to explain to a child such as yourself. All you have to do is follow orders. Aim and push the button. Surely even you can do something that simple. The Super Wings bicycle will be yours. Just think, this one little job could turn everything around for you. I would think that would be a fairly good offer for a boy everyone is calling Rotten-Egg Smedlowe."

Barry looked down in shame and anger, remembering his humiliation from yesterday.

"I could show everybody I wasn't rotten, couldn't I?" Barry asked. His eyes began to dance. "I could even show Sloan I'm somebody to be taken seriously."

"You could indeed," Captain Sharp said. "Do you accept this mission?"

"You bet!" Barry said in a voice of both triumph and desperation. "I'll do anything. When do we start?"

"Right now," the Captain said as he opened the passenger door to the black jeep. Barry got inside eagerly.

They drove at once out toward the west of town. They went down Cemetery Road, past the big Goliath factory, the country club, and the new Security Squad Center. Barry wondered if Josh and Randy were still inside. But Captain Sharp kept going, passing into the large stretch of forest. They rode past fields and a few farmhouses and then turned onto a smaller dirt road. They rode a few miles before the jeep stopped.

"The farmhouse and children are up ahead and down the driveway on your right," Captain Sharp said.

"I know where it is," Barry said. "Let's just get this over with."

"I like your enthusiasm," Captain Sharp said. He took the brand-new golden Super Wings bicycle out of the jeep. Barry hopped on. The Captain gave him the black Nega-Cam camera.

"Don't dawdle," Captain Sharp said. His eyes were watery and bright. "And don't let them see you."

"I'm going," Barry grunted. He began pedaling down the dirt road. He looked back once. The Captain waved for him to go forward. Barry passed an old rusty mailbox and turned into the gravel driveway of the Kramar place. As he got closer he could see that the workshop doors were open. Barry got off the bike and laid it down in some tall brown weeds. He crept toward the workshop. Just as he was about to enter, he heard noises from the inside. Barry ran to hide around the corner of the workshop building. Then he peeked around the corner. John Kramar came outside first, pushing his old red Spirit Flyer bicycle. He was followed by over thirty other children and their bikes. No one seemed to notice Barry.

Barry lifted up the Nega-Cam and peered through the lens. All the children were down on one knee and seemed to be talking softly. Barry stared at them. He wondered what they were doing. He was about to press the little black trigger button when three tall men in white clothes suddenly appeared between him and the Spirit Flyer people. Barry was sure they hadn't been there before. He blinked and lifted up his head. The men who had come out of nowhere looked right at Barry. They stepped toward him. He screamed out in fear and surprise.

"Aaaaaack!" Barry yelled. The men didn't appear angry, but they didn't seem too friendly either. In fact, Barry wasn't sure that they were men at all. They seemed to almost glow in their white clothes.

Barry tried to aim the camera. One of the men reached out and touched the Nega-Cam. The black camera began to vibrate and twist in his hands so it was aimed at himself just as Barry pressed the trigger button.

A blinding electric flash burst out of the Nega-Cam. Barry was plunged into darkness. He couldn't see a thing. Barry had been blinded by a camera flash before, but this time it was different. He expected his eyes to adjust in a few seconds, but he remained blind. The Nega-Cam was no longer in his hands. He reached for his eyes. His eyelids were open, but he still couldn't see.

"I can't see. I can't see!" Barry yelled out. "I'm blind. Help me!" He swirled around and started to run but heard a dull clank near his chest. Barry reached for the sound. Another surge of fear shot through the boy as he felt a large chain hanging there. Barry jerked the chain and tried to throw it off. But it was locked to his neck. Barry was about to pull it again when the chain suddenly jerked him off his feet. Barry fell down and was dragged across the ground. He grabbed the chain with both hands and pulled back with all his might, but something stronger was on the other end.

The dragging chain suddenly pulled the boy deeper into his blindness. He felt his feet leaving the earth. "Stop!" the boy pleaded, but the chain kept pulling him through the darkness. Barry felt dizzy. His heart pounded wildly. He was sure he was going to die. Then suddenly the pulling stopped.

His sight slowly returned to his opened eyes. He blinked because he seemed to be looking at himself. He was in a very dim room. The walls seemed to be made of blue smoke. Right in front of him was a giant of a boy standing behind a huge gray metal desk. The boy wore a gray ORDER uniform. But Barry stared at his face because it looked just like his own face, only stiff, as if it was a kind of mask. Then the gigantic figure laughed a loud braying laugh that sounded like a sick donkey with hiccups. Barry recognized his own voice. The gigantic figure was holding Barry's chain which looked as tiny as a dog leash in the over-sized hand. With another laugh, he yanked the chain and Barry stumbled forward until he was right in front of the desk.

"Welcome to the Centerville Bureau of Children and Parent Relations," the gigantic Barry sneered. "You finally graduated, traitor boy."

"I did what?" Barry asked in a cracking voice.

"Bring out the scales!" the gigantic Barry roared, ignoring his question. "Let's judge this rotten slimeball and get it over with—I'm hungry."

Barry was too shocked and surprised to speak. Behind him, he heard a creaking noise. He turned and saw four more child-creatures in gray ORDER uniforms pushing an old-fashioned set of balance scales. They looked just like the kind of scales that Mrs. Johnson used in science class, only they were huge, over twenty feet tall. The four children pushed the scales right behind Barry and stopped. That's when Barry noticed that the tallest and biggest of the four had a face just like Sloan Favor. The other creatures resembled Jason, Alvin and Roger Darrow.

"So Rotten-Egg Smedlowe is ready to fry," the Sloan-creature said, with a laugh. The voice sounded just like Sloan's. Barry didn't see how the person could be Sloan, yet it seemed so much like him.

Barry looked at the scales. There were two large metal dishes hanging in the balance. On one side, the word *GOOD* was written on the dish. On the other dish was written the word *EVIL*.

"Hop up, traitor boy," the large Barry grunted and then snickered.

"What do you mean?" Barry asked.

"I mean get up on the scales, stupid," the giant roared. "It's time to weigh in."

Barry looked uneasily at the scales. He still wasn't sure what to do. With a disgusted sneer, the gigantic Barry lifted up his hand that held the chain. Barry felt himself being pulled up into the air. With a flick of his wrist, the giant placed Barry directly over the dish labeled *EVIL* and dropped him. Barry hit the dish and that side of the scales immediately sank to the ground. Up at the top of the scales there was a dull clanking sound and a word in dark purple letters lit up that spelled *GUILTY.*

"Guilty, just as I thought," the gigantic Barry figure grunted. "Of course everyone in the whole town knows you're a guilty rotten-egg of a kid. It's ashes time for you, buddy boy. I'm just surprised they didn't cash in your chain sooner. Send him away!"

"Wait a minute," Barry said. "There's nothing in the other side of the scales. That's not fair."

"Some stupid boys never learn," the giant scowled. With a groan, he lifted Barry up over to the other side of the scales. Then he dropped him down in the dish labeled *GOOD.* Nothing happened. The dish stayed high in the air. Up above, the purple words were the same: *GUILTY.*

"Same old story," the gigantic Barry said and laughed. "I told you it was ashes time. It's been nice knowing you, kid. You fed me well."

"But it's not true!" Barry didn't understand it all, but he knew he had just been judged and found wanting. "I'm not totally guilty. I . . . I am good, I'm . . ."

"Ask them if it's not true," the gigantic Barry said. "They are my witnesses."

Barry looked behind him. He was surprised to see three tall men dressed in white clothes. They were the same men he had seen at the Kramar farm. They were the ones who had blocked him from using the Nega-Cam.

"Is he guilty or not?" the gigantic Barry asked the three men.

They nodded silently.

"And do I own his chain or not?" the gigantic Barry asked.

The three men nodded silently again.

"Then it's ashes time," the gigantic Barry said. He stood up and walked from behind a desk. Barry hadn't seen it before, but there was a long hall just off to one side behind the desk. As the gigantic figure walked toward the hall, he pulled the dark chain. Barry was yanked off the scales and dragged behind. The gigantic figure entered the hall. As they went in, Barry looked up. There were words written right above the entrance of the hall that said, Smedlowe, Barry; Centerville. Barry's eyes went wide with fear when he saw flames down at the far end of the hall. A very hot fire seemed to be burning there. The gigantic figure started walking toward the fire, dragging Barry by his chain. The Sloan-creature followed them eagerly.

"What's that fire?" Barry asked.

"Ashes time," the uniformed figure said laughing loudly.

"Help!" Barry yelled when he realized what was happening. The three men in white clothes suddenly moved from behind the scales all the way in front of the gigantic Barry, blocking his way.

"Out of my way," the giant figure hissed. "You saw what the scales said."

"But he cried for help," said one of the men. "He has a right to see the rooms and change his mind."

"He's history," the giant said in scorn.

One of the three men suddenly held a large white sword in his hand. The gigantic figures stared at the sword, their eyes glowing red with anger.

"He has a right to see the rooms," the man repeated. "You know the rules. He may wake up. He still has a chance to be cured of his blindness."

"He's a rotten egg all the way through," the large Sloan figure sneered.

"I'll see you at the end of the hall. This is one rotten egg I can't wait to see fried."

The Sloan figure walked down the hall, laughing loudly as he walked into the flames. The large Barry figure walked after him. The dark chain stretched out behind him and seemed to grow longer, though one end was still connected to the heavy metal collar around Barry's neck. The gigantic figure kept walking and walked right into the fire at the end of the hall, disappearing into the flames. For a moment, Barry realized his fate had been delayed.

The men in white clothes looked at Barry. The one with the drawn sword came over and took Barry's hand.

"You must pass by the rooms," the man said, holding Barry's hand.

"Pass by the rooms?" Barry asked. He wondered what the man meant. Then he looked down the hall again. One side of the hall was a plain wall, but on the other side were open rooms. Far down at the end of the hall was the waiting fire. He was about to ask another question, when the three men faded and then disappeared as he watched. Yet, somehow they didn't seem to be gone. Just then, his chain pulled him forward. Though Barry felt alone, he also felt something else in the long hall with him. Not knowing what else to do, he began walking down the hall, the chain clanking at his feet. He felt like he had started the longest journey of his life.

THE ROOMS OF JUDGMENT

16

Barry stopped in front of the first room. Immediately the room lit up. Yet it was more than light. Barry had a sense that the room woke up, as if it had been asleep. It almost seemed like a room in a museum, with the chair and desk and bed. Yet this room was very familiar because it was a lot like his room at home. Barry rubbed his eyes. For a moment, he wasn't sure it was just a copy of his room, but his actual room itself. He was pondering that when the bedroom door opened. Barry was amazed when he saw himself walk in. Only he was much younger. He figured this Barry was around eight years old. Then much to his surprise, his brother Bobby walked into the room. Bobby was carrying a sleeping bag as well as a duffle bag.

"I'm telling you it's true," Bobby said to the younger Barry. "It's an old red bike and it flies. I even took a ride on it."

"You're lying to me," the little Barry said. There was the sound of a honking horn. "You've got to go to camp now. They're waiting in the car."

"I'll show you when I get back," Bobby said. "You'll believe me then, once you take a ride."

"I'll never believe you, Bobby," the little Barry said firmly. "You're a liar."

Bobby started to answer, but the car horn honked again. His brother looked at Barry with frustration. But just then, Barry saw someone or something else in the room, almost like a ghost. It was that same creature that wore a mask of himself, only the creature was smaller. The creature then did an odd thing. He took two dark round pieces of something that looked like black plastic and he placed them over each of Barry's eyes so Barry looked blind. Then the creature disappeared and the black eye-coverings seemed to fade at the same time, covering the boy's eyes with an invisible shadow.

"You're just mad because you can't come to camp with me," Bobby said. "But I'll show you I'm not a liar when I get back." Bobby went out the door. The lights in the room slowly went out.

"Don't go," Barry said softly. "I didn't mean to call you a liar." But Bobby was gone. Barry remembered feeling bad the day Bobby went to camp, but he had forgotten that they had argued.

The lights in the next room woke up. Barry was pulled forward by his chain until he stopped in front of the room. This time they were at the Centerville Cemetery. People were standing around crying. Barry immediately recognized that it was the day of Bobby's funeral. Everyone looked sad. Barry saw himself in the little black suit he had worn only that one time. His parents were among a group of his relatives. Josh and Randy were standing off to one side looking solemnly at the hole in the ground. Two old men began to shovel dirt into the grave. Barry saw his eight-year-old self cry out.

"You lied and tricked me, Bobby," the eight-year-old Barry yelled angrily and began to run. He ran and ran and ran, past the graves, past the old trees until he was stopped by the old iron fence. He leaned against its bars, sobbing. Then Barry saw someone else watching. It was a man, but unlike any other man Barry had seen, though at the same time Barry was sure he had seen him before. He had a very kind face and wore a golden crown, like a prince. The man came over and touched the sobbing little boy on the shoulder. Soon after, Barry's father walked over and looked down at his son. His father just watched in silence. He didn't see the man with the golden crown. The lights dimmed in that room.

Barry blinked back tears, remembering that day. More than anything, he had felt angry at Bobby for dying. He had felt tricked and abandoned. The lights came on in the next room. Barry shuffled forward, wondering what he would see there.

He saw a classroom full of kids. Benny Bradley, a very popular boy who had been in Barry's third-grade class, was handing out little envelopes. Barry immediately remembered that they were invitations to Benny's birthday. The kids stood in a group around Benny, smiling eagerly as he handed out invitations. Barry saw himself in the group of children. Every child got an invitation except Barry. Barry waited.

"My mom must have forgotten your invitation," Benny said uneasily.

"You didn't want me to come," little Barry said as Benny walked away. Barry stormed out of the room as he fought back the tears.

"He lied to me," Barry said, as the lights faded. He could remember that day as well as yesterday, the anger and humiliation of being the only one left out.

The lights came on in the next room. Barry saw his kitchen at home. He was sitting at a table writing down a list of names on a piece of paper. His mother was beside him.

"Did you forget to put Benny Bradley on your list for your birthday party?" his mother asked.

"He can't come to my party," Barry said firmly. "I don't want to have a party if he comes."

"Are you sure?" his mother asked. "You know Bobby was a good friend of Benny's older brother."

"He can't come to my party," Barry repeated. "I'll never forget what he did to me." The boy's face was as hard as stone. Then another person appeared in the room. It was the creature that looked like Barry, only his face was like a mask. He took a long black snake and dropped it on little Barry's lap. The ghostlike snake immediately coiled around the boy's arm and bit down into Barry's shoulder. The lights in the room went out.

Barry walked down the hall. As he passed the next room, the lights revealed another scene in Barry's past. Barry remembered it right away. It was the summer after third grade.

He was at the baseball field. It was a regular season game in the last inning. Barry was at bat and all the people were yelling and cheering. Runners were on second and third base. His team was one run behind.

"Smedlowe at bat for the Wildcats," the announcer said. "Number 23, Bobby Smedlowe. I mean, Barry Smedlowe, excuse me, son."

Young Barry cringed at the announcer's mistake. He suddenly felt very much afraid and on the spot. His brother Bobby had been an excellent batter. Barry swung hard at the first pitch and missed. The second pitch was a called strike. And on the third pitch, Barry swung as hard as he ever had. He was sure he was going to hit a home run, but he didn't even touch the ball.

"Strike three, you're out!" the umpire yelled and the game was over. Barry walked dejectedly back to the dugout. His father was in the stands. Barry looked at him, and his father just shook his head sadly. Barry kicked at the dirt.

"Bobby Smedlowe wouldn't have struck out," a teammate said with disgust. Barry sat on the bench in the dugout until everyone left. The lights went out on the scene. Barry stood looking into the darkness.

In the next scene Barry saw his room. He was in his baseball uniform that same evening.

"Are you sure you want to quit the team?" Mr. Smedlowe said. Barry nodded silently, not looking at his father.

"I don't understand. Your brother Bobby never quit anything in his life," Mr. Smedlowe said. "He was a player, not a quitter." His dad left the room. Barry watched himself sitting on the bed. This time he saw that the same dark chain and metal collar were around his neck. The chain faded as the lights in the room went out.

Barry kept moving down the hall, pulled by his chain in front of each room, staring back into his past. He didn't want to look, but he knew he had to. He couldn't walk by those rooms without looking. But when he looked, he felt the pain of each memory all over again. And with the pain, he felt his old anger burning hotter inside, consuming him. As he walked, his legs grew heavier and heavier. He began to dread looking inside the rooms, afraid of what he would see. Yet he had to pass them. There was no way to avoid them. The fire at the end of the hall still seemed far away. Yet that's where Barry knew he would end his journey, walking into the flames because that's where the chain was pulling him.

As he walked, the next series of rooms became bitter. He saw himself at school hurting people, sometimes in little ways, sometimes in big ways. One room showed him and a bunch of other kids on the stairs at school. Roger Darrow walked in front of Barry. Roger had not chosen Barry to be on his softball team the recess before, even though Barry had wanted Roger to pick him. As they were going down the stairs, Barry stuck his foot in front of Roger's legs. Roger tumbled down the stairs and landed in a shriek. As it turned out, Roger had sprained his arm. Barry had always remembered with satisfaction the sound of Roger's scream and the sight of him in pain. Barry had avoided getting in trouble since no one really saw him trip Roger. But watching it this time, Barry saw how badly Roger had been hurt.

"Well, he deserved it," Barry muttered. But he knew it wasn't true. Barry walked past more rooms, the rooms where he had caused other children pain or embarrassment. He had tripped them, pulled their hair, torn up their papers, told lies about them to teachers and called them ugly names. There seemed to be no end to these rooms where he had caused other people pain. Sometimes Barry saw himself covered with the half-invisible dark chain and biting snakes. Sometimes he saw that shadowy creature with his face. But what he noticed most was the pain he had caused others. And the more he looked, the more guilty he felt. He tried to make excuses, saying they deserved what they got, or it was all a mistake, but deep inside Barry knew better. The excuses didn't erase the facts of what he had done. Even though he had always avoided getting in trouble at the time he had done these things, Barry saw that the facts and the guilt had remained with him.

Barry stopped in front of a more recent room that really scared him. He saw himself riding an old red Spirit Flyer bicycle down the street at night. Actually, he wasn't riding it, but being taken for a ride by it. Barry had tried to steal the old red Spirit Flyer bike from John Kramar with the help of a mysterious man named Horace Grinsby. But as Barry had tried to hit the old bike with a hammer, to destroy it, the bike had moved all by itself, taking Barry for a wild ride down the streets of Centerville. The ride had ended when Barry got dumped in a hole full of sewer water. The boy shuddered when he saw himself running home down the dark streets, soaked and wet with shame. He looked away.

He still had to pass by the rooms. They just seemed to get worse: more lies, more acts of vengeance and betrayals, the memories of fear and anger. None of the rooms had been lost. Then Barry came to a room he dreaded. He was making a deal with Captain Sharp to turn in Josh and Randy. Barry had to watch the whole thing. Even though he tried to turn away his head, he had to stare into Josh's eyes once more as his cousin was taken from his house by the men from ORDER. Little Randy shrieked out in fear all over again.

"I didn't mean to," Barry moaned, falling to his knees, his eyes filling with tears. Yet he had to keep looking. The longer he stayed in front of this room, the worse it became. All the guilt and fear and pain had accumulated in his walk past the rooms. Through blurry eyes he saw his chain leading into the burning fire. Then Barry realized he was truly destined for ashes and that he would not escape the flames because he was a slave. He was guilty and everyone knew it. There seemed to be no way out of this place of darkness in his soul. He felt alone and abandoned in the rooms he had made for himself. The boy watched in horror as Josh and Randy were dragged off again.

"What have I done?" Barry cried out. "Josh, I'm sorry. Randy, I'm sorry. I'm sorry. I'm sorry, everyone. I'm so sorry. I've hurt everyone. I can't look anymore. Stop it!"

Barry hung his head and wept. All the rooms and scenes kept flashing before him. The waves of shame and guilt seemed overpowering, as if they would suffocate him. Barry didn't think he could cry hard enough to expel the pain he was feeling. The chain kept pulling him toward the flames. He felt that it was useless to resist.

The room in front of him changed. Josh and Randy were still there, but they were in a different place, a drab gray room with two little beds. Bars were across the only window in the room. It reminded Barry of a jail cell. Both Josh and Randy were kneeling by their beds and talking to themselves, it seemed. But then, Barry saw someone else in the room. The two boys weren't alone at all. At first Barry thought the other person was one of those men in white, but this person was different. He seemed important, very important. It was the man with the golden crown, the one who looked like a prince. And the more Barry watched, the stronger and more powerful this man appeared. Josh and Randy didn't seem to notice this important man, even though they appeared to be talking right to him. Then Barry heard the words.

"Oh, Kingson, Prince of the universe, forgive my cousin Barry for what he did to us," Josh said. "Take away his blindness and forgive him. Show him the way out. Show him who you are."

"I forgive Barry, Kingson," Randy said in his small voice. "Forgive Barry, please."

The words cut into Barry's heart. He felt the tears coming again. But then the important man in the room, the Kingson, looked up, straight into Barry's eyes. Besides his shame, the boy immediately felt a great fear. Just then, the creature with Barry's face came staggering out of the flames, dragging the huge set of scales.

"He's mine!" the figure shouted. "You saw the verdict. Guilty! Even the boy knows. A grasshopper has more good points to his account than this boy."

The important man, the Kingson, remained, still staring at Barry. He hardly seemed to hear his accuser, but stared at Barry. The boy felt more ashamed and afraid than ever because he knew that this strange and wonderful person knew him more than he knew himself.

"Don't be afraid of those who can destroy your body," the Kingson said solemnly. "But fear the one who can destroy your body and soul as well."

The Kingson seemed to be closer. He moved out of the room and into the hall.

"I want out of here," Barry said. "I'm sorry for all the things I did. I want out of here. Can you help me?"

"The scales," the gigantic Barry creature shouted. "He's guilty and you know it."

"Stand on the scales," the Kingson commanded. Barry was too afraid not to climb up on the big round dish once more. And once again, the scales tipped against him. The word at the top was *GUILTY,* in big purple letters.

"See, I told you," the gigantic Barry creature whined. "He's guilty, Guilty, GUILTY!"

"I have gold to pay his ransom," the Kingson said. The Kingson reached into a pouch hanging on his belt. The pouch seemed to have red stains on it, like blood. But when he pulled out his hand, he was holding four gold coins.

"Do you want my gold, the gold of my goodness?" the Kingson asked Barry.

"Yes, yes," Barry said eagerly.

"Are you worthy to receive it?" the Kingson asked.

Barry wanted to say yes more than anything in his life, but he realized he couldn't lie and look this man in the eyes. Barry bowed his head in shame. He knew he didn't deserve such a gift.

"No, I'm not," Barry said softly.

Barry could barely believe it when he looked up and the Kingson was holding out his hands with the gold coins toward him. Barry dropped to his knees. He cautiously opened his hands. The Kingson let the gold coins drop into Barry's hands.

As soon as they touched his hands, Barry was sure he would drop the coins because they were so heavy. His whole body seemed over-whelmed by their weight and glory as they sparkled and shone. Imme-diately the balance of the scales changed. Barry was surprised when he looked up at the top of the scales. The word was no longer *GUILTY*. Now it said *FREE*.

"Noooooo!" howled the creature with Barry's face. "He's still mine. I own the chain. He's a slave to the domain of darkness. He belongs here." With that, he yanked and Barry felt the weight on his neck as the collar ring pulled tight.

"Do you want to stay here, or be a subject in my kingdom?" the Prince asked Barry. "Think carefully. You will be free in my kingdom, yet you will be my subject, and I will be your king. What do you say? Who do you want to own your life? You must chose between this domain or me."

"I want you, your majesty," Barry said without hesitation. And with those words, he bowed down until his face was touching the metal dish of the balance scale. And as he leaned over, something like pieces of black plastic fell off his eyes. Barry blinked in surprise. Everything was suddenly lighter and clearer, as if he had been wearing dark sunglasses until just that moment and yet not realized it.

He looked up at the Kingson with new eyes. No sooner had he lifted his head than Barry saw the Prince of kings lift a sword and swing it down right into the dark chain. There was a flash and the crack of thunder as the chain broke beneath the blade. The collar ring and chain fell off in a jangle.

"Nooooooo!" the creature with Barry's face howled once again. It had been pulling on the chain and fell backward, off-balance, into the fire. At once the flames began to consume the gray creature as it screamed in agony.

"Come with me," the Prince of Kings said with a smile. "Let me show you my kingdom."

He took Barry's hand. The room in front of them was no longer just a room but a long hall, filled with light. And as they walked into it, Barry realized he had found a way out of the domain of darkness. He was freed from the long dark chain of his past.

Up ahead of him the light got brighter. Barry's heart pounded with joy and excitement and anticipation as the hallway widened. Then it opened into a great expanse that Barry couldn't begin to describe. The kingdom was filled with a music of a kind that he had never heard before. But as he joined in the songs, a great lightness was released in his heart. Barry was still singing as he finally headed toward his home.

AN APOLOGY
OFFERED
• • • • • • • •

17

Barry flew home that night on an old red
bicycle just as it was getting dark. While in the kingdom, he had received, from the hands of the Prince of Kings himself, a big red Spirit
Flyer bicycle. Though the bicycle looked old and somewhat worn, Barry
immediately realized what a treasure he had when he was shown how
to ride it. He flew up in the skies of the wonderful kingdom, carried
on the waves of a hundred beautiful songs.

He was anxious to tell his parents about his new bike and adventures,
but they weren't home. His mom had left a note on the refrigerator
saying she and his father had gone to a very important town meeting

with the people from ORDER and all the state and local officials.

Barry sat on his old red bicycle out in the garage, remembering the events of the day. He was still bathed in the glow of both sorrow and gladness, having met the Kingson and having been freed from the chain. For the first time in a long time, Barry didn't feel that heaviness and fear biting into him.

When he walked upstairs to go to bed, Barry noticed the door to Bobby's old room was open. He peeked inside and saw Josh and Randy's school books on the bed. Barry felt tears come to his eyes, remembering Josh and Randy. More than anything, he wished he could see them so he could tell them how sorry he was and to ask their forgiveness.

For the first time since he could remember, Barry slept well and easily. He had exciting dreams all night of riding the old red Spirit Flyer bicycle. He woke up happy.

He looked out the window and saw dark cold clouds covering the town, threatening rain or snow. A storm had blown in during the night. But that didn't stop Barry. He went downstairs excitedly, still wearing his pajamas.

His parents were drinking coffee at the table. They looked tired and worn out, as if they hadn't slept. Barry stared at them and smiled. His mother sighed when she saw him. His father seemed uneasy. Barry was disappointed. He thought they would be as happy as he felt.

"Isn't this a great day?" Barry asked enthusiastically.

"I thought you'd still be in a bad mood about those rotten eggs," Mr. Smedlowe said. "I thought you'd be mad for two weeks."

"I'd forgotten all about that," Barry replied. Though it had only happened two days before, it seemed like a year. "Do you think we can get Josh and Randy home today?"

His parents were quiet. They stared at their coffee. Mrs. Smedlowe sniffled. "We'll be fortunate to get them at all," Mrs. Smedlowe said wiping her eyes. "And they may be the least of our worries. We'll be lucky if we all don't end up in jail or some Security Squad camp."

"What do you mean?" Barry asked.

"Your mother is upset," Mr. Smedlowe said slowly. "The city council meeting last night didn't go well. The new ORDER government is putting all kinds of new rules and laws into effect, starting today. The new Point System is going on line fully. It's finally working. All good citizens are supposed to register with their new number cards. I'm not sure what the penalty is if you don't register, but they're making a big deal out of it. The government is also going to make changes in the school system. If you aren't registered in the Point System officially, you can't go to school. They're also putting a lot of pressure on us personally because of Josh and Randy and the election."

"They're putting pressure on everyone who doesn't just agree with them totally," Mrs. Smedlowe said. "They won't even discuss things. They're like dictators!"

"Well, a lot of people agree with them," his father said. "There have been a lot of incidents of looting and riots this week farther down state and people are scared. They don't want that happening here."

"But I don't like being threatened and forced to go along with them," Mrs. Smedlowe replied. "Everyone is supposed to register today with their new number cards down at the courthouse. You get more bonus points the sooner you do it. They have a new gigantic Big Board set up. A lot of people registered last night. But other people said they would never register. I think they're right. This country used to be a democracy. We used to be able to disagree without being threatened by the government."

"Well, the government has changed," Mr. Smedlowe said glumly. "We may not like it, but they got the majority of votes. We have to obey the new laws or face a possible fine or jail sentence. A lot of the old-timers were really mad at the meeting last night. I thought there'd be a riot right there."

"But there were so many of those ORDER Security Squad people there. They were ready for a riot," Mrs. Smedlowe said. "I don't understand why they have to have so many guns. It's like they suspect the normal citizens of Centerville of being criminals."

"It's just the fear people are feeling," Mr. Smedlowe said.

"Well, I'm not afraid," Barry said, trying to sound brave. "I mean, I'm not afraid now. I was scared until yesterday, but then a wonderful thing happened to me. I was trying to do a mean thing, but I was blinded. Then I was pulled into this dark place by my chain. I thought they would keep me there forever, but the Kingson paid for my freedom with four gold coins and cut the chain off me with his sword. And then I got a Spirit Flyer bicycle and it was all just wonderful!"

"What did you say?" Mr. Smedlowe asked. His father seemed puzzled by Barry's happy outburst.

Barry quickly tried to explain what had happened to him as well as he could. Only he was talking so fast, trying not to leave anything out, that he seemed to confuse his parents. The more he told them, the more puzzled and surprised they seemed.

"And I got a Spirit Flyer bicycle, just like Josh and Randy, and like Bobby used to have," Barry said. "Come look."

Barry ran to open the door that led out to the garage. His parents followed him. Mr. Smedlowe frowned when he saw the old red bicycle leaning against his workbench.

"You're sure that's not Josh's bike?" Mr. Smedlowe asked. "You didn't steal it?"

"Of course I didn't steal it," Barry said. "You can't steal a Spirit Flyer, believe me."

His parents stared at the old bicycle. His mother put her hand up to her mouth. "We'll have to hide it or get rid of it," Mrs. Smedlowe said.

"What?" Barry asked dumbfounded.

"You're probably right," Mr. Smedlowe added. He walked over and got a tarp off the shelf above the workbench. He unfolded it and covered the Spirit Flyer with it. "We're in enough trouble as it is."

"But you can't," Barry yelled, rushing toward his bike. He pulled off the tarp. "I just got this bike. They do really neat things. They can take you into the presence of the Prince of Kings himself."

"Come inside, Barry," Mr. Smedlowe said. "I'll tell you why we are concerned."

From the look on his parents' faces, Barry knew he should listen. He didn't protest when his father pulled the tarp back over the bicycle. He followed them inside. His mother poured more coffee into his dad's cup. Mr. Smedlowe cleared his throat after taking a sip.

"At the meeting last night, the people from ORDER were particularly hard on those people who had Spirit Flyer bicycles," Mr. Smedlowe said. "It wasn't only them, but they were included as one group considered subversive to the government."

"Subversive to the government?" Barry asked. "What does that mean?"

"They see certain groups as being dangerous to the new government, or possibly against the government," Mr. Smedlowe said.

"You mean like traitors?" Barry asked.

"Yes, in a way," Mr. Smedlowe said. "It's not only those people with Spirit Flyers but lots of other people. Certain groups are being singled out. Anyone who didn't vote for ORDER in this last election is looked on as being possibly dangerous. I don't think that's true, but a lot of people who are afraid are listening to this scare talk from the ORDER government. People with Spirit Flyers are easily recognizable, especially since they were quite vocal about their disagreements with the ORDER candidates. That's why it's not wise for you to be riding that bike right now or letting others know we have one in this house. We're already under enough suspicion as it is. Having that bike around just makes it worse."

"But Dad, you don't understand what a Spirit Flyer can do!"

"I don't understand a lot of things," Mr. Smedlowe replied, cleaning his glasses nervously with a handkerchief. "After this blows over, things will get better, I'm sure. We'll talk about it then."

"But what if it doesn't blow over?" Barry asked.

His parents were quiet. The stillness was broken by the telephone ringing.

Mr. Smedlowe answered it in the other room. He talked awhile. When he returned, he looked pale.

"Your mother and I need to go out right away," he said. "I'll explain it later. Just don't ride that bike, do you understand?"

Barry nodded despondently. He felt left out as his parents got their coats and rushed out the front door. He watched them drive away. He was about to close the door when he saw Roger Darrow and two other boys zoom down the street and stop in front of Sloan Favor's house across the street. Sloan came out of the garage, pushing his bike. The boys zoomed back down the street toward town. They seemed to be in a hurry. Barry was curious.

He quickly ate a sliced-up banana with his cereal and then raced upstairs to get dressed. He ran to the garage. He pulled back the tarp from the old bicycle and stared at it. He was strongly tempted to ignore his father's command. Yet when he sat down in the seat, something inside him didn't feel right. The old, chained Barry would have just sneaked the bike out and ridden it. But this Barry had changed. He got off the bike and started to cover it up when he saw something hanging on the handlebars. Barry leaned over and picked up an old pair of goggles. They looked just like old aviator goggles. Stuck in the center between the two eyepieces were three tiny gold crowns. On the straps of the goggles were the words *Spirit Flyer Vision*. Barry knew deep inside that even if he had to leave the bike, he could take the goggles. He put them in his pocket and left the house, making sure the door was locked.

Barry walked toward the downtown square of Centerville. As he got closer he began to run, though he wasn't sure why. He could sense a tension in the air. Barry noticed other people moving toward the square also. When he got to Main Street and Eighth Street, two blocks from the square, he stopped.

John and Susan Kramar and a bunch of other kids were sitting on their Spirit Flyer bicycles looking down toward the square. Then John saw Barry. Barry smiled, but John didn't look too happy. Barry walked over, smiling. The other children stared at him coldly.

"What trick are you trying to pull today?" John Kramar asked as Barry walked up.

"I'm not pulling any tricks," Barry said, feeling slightly confused. He had hoped the others would be happy to see him. "I just came to tell you I got a Spirit Flyer bike too."

"If you have a bike, then why aren't you riding it?" Daniel Bayley asked. He looked straight into Barry's eyes.

"Well, I would have, but my parents told me I couldn't ride it today," Barry said, beginning to feel frustrated. He wanted to show them he was their friend. "I'm glad I saw you because I wanted to tell you I'm sorry for trying to spy on you yesterday. I was wrong."

John didn't seem to even be listening. He was looking down toward the square. But Susan was staring straight at Barry.

"Why are you sorry?" Susan asked.

"Because it was wrong," Barry said. "I tried to do a sneaky thing. I'm sorry. I'm sorry for all of the mean things I've done, and I want to apologize to you all."

John looked at Barry silently. He was still waiting for some trick.

"Let's get closer to see what's going on," John said to the other kids on the bikes.

"Do you think we should?" Amy Burke asked. "My mom said people were acting pretty angry and upset last night."

"Sure," John said. "I'm not afraid. We can always get away." The children on the old red Spirit Flyer bikes began to pedal down the street toward the square. Barry ran after them.

"Don't you believe I'm sorry?" Barry asked, as he trotted alongside John, trying to keep up.

"Why should we believe you?" John asked. "You say you have a Spirit

Flyer, yet I don't see you riding it. And anyone can say they are sorry and not mean it."

"But I am sorry!" Barry said, feeling more frustrated than ever. "Yesterday, I was blinded when I tried to use that weird camera Captain Sharp gave me. I couldn't see, but I got dragged by my chain into this dark place. When I finally could see, some big ugly creatures with masks over their faces said they owned me because of the chain. But some other strange men in white clothes helped me out. They showed me all the things I had done in these rooms. It was like I was a slave to the chain and never saw it. The chain was dragging me into this awful fire, but the Kingson gave me gold coins and broke my chain so I was free. Then he gave me a Spirit Flyer. It was wonderful!"

Susan stared over at Barry as they pedaled. She seemed interested. "Maybe he did get free from his chain," Susan said to John. She stopped her bike. John stopped and the other kids stopped. "He must have seen the Aggeloi and Daimones."

"He could just be making it up to fool us," John said tersely. He looked at Barry in disgust. "After all, he was trying to spy on us yesterday. And look what he did to Josh and Randy, his own family."

Barry looked down at the mention of his cousins. He felt himself getting embarrassed. He didn't know what to do or say to make John and the other kids believe he had changed.

"I'm sorry for doing that too," Barry said softly, feeling the tears coming to his eyes.

"You don't need to apologize to me," John Kramar grunted. "They're the ones in trouble. If you were really sorry, you'd apologize to them, not that it does any good now."

Barry didn't have anything to say. John's words cut deeply into him.

"I will say I'm sorry when I get the chance," Barry said finally, almost on the verge of tears. "And I'll try to make it up to them."

"Talk is easy," John said, not hiding his annoyance as he stared at Barry. The other children were quiet. Barry looked at the ground. In a lot of ways, he knew John was right. It was easy to say something, but the hard part was doing what you said you would do. And Barry wasn't sure how he could make things right with Josh and Randy.

Just then, the sound of a scream split the air. Noises of shouting came from the square. After a few moments, the noise settled down. "Maybe we should get out of here," Susan said. "That scream makes me nervous."

"Are you kidding?" John said. "I'm going to investigate." John stood up on his pedals and raced down Main Street toward the noise. Susan frowned but pedaled after her cousin anyway. Amy and Daniel and the other kids on the bikes all followed. Barry watched them. Then he ran toward the square to find out what was going on.

AT THE
TOWN SQUARE
. . . .
18

Barry ran faster to catch up with the other kids, hoping some of his frustration would go away. He had been sure John Kramar and the other kids with Spirit Flyers would be glad to welcome him into their midst, but they all seemed suspicious or afraid of him. He felt so different and wonderful, but no one seemed to believe him or care. His new-found joy was beginning to fade.

The kids with Spirit Flyer bikes had stopped on the south side of the square away from the corner and close to an alley. Barry stood behind John and Susan to watch. The square was filled with people. On every corner, four or five men and women in gray ORDER Security Squad uniforms were standing at attention with guns strapped over their backs. The men in ORDER uniforms frowned at the children on the Spirit Flyer bikes.

The center of the square was especially crowded with people. Most of them were in a long line that led into the courthouse. Many were holding things. From a distance, Barry could tell they were holding number cards.

"They are all registering with their number cards," Susan Kramar said. "I don't think Dad plans to register, even though they made it like a law. It's in effect over the whole state. He sounded real upset last night."

Just then, Captain Sharp's black jeep came down Tenth Street from the west and entered the square. He drove slowly around the square once and then parked in front of the courthouse. A few moments later, Sloan Favor and his gang came riding down Tenth Street as if they had followed Captain Sharp. There were over fifty children on their shiny Super Wings bicycles. They all wore gray Commando uniforms. Sloan and many of the children were carrying paper bags. They parked their bikes and got in line to register. Some were holding their number cards. Barry stared at the bags curiously. He wondered what was inside. Captain Sharp walked quickly up the steps of the courthouse and disappeared inside.

"I wonder what's really going on?" John Kramar asked.

"Maybe these will help," Amy Burke said. She took out a pair of old goggles that looked like aviator goggles. They looked just like the ones Barry had found on his Spirit Flyer bicycle that morning. They had the same sign of the Three Crowns in the center panel and the name *Spirit Flyer Vision*. Amy slipped the goggles on and stared at the courthouse.

"I have some of those," Barry said.

"You do?" John Kramar asked with surprise.

"Yeah, I found them this morning," Barry said. "They were on the handlebars of my Spirit Flyer bike. See?"

Barry pulled the goggles out of his pocket. John leaned over and immediately saw the sign of the Three Crowns. He frowned.

"May I look at them?" Susan asked Barry. He gave her the goggles. She too looked closely at the little golden sign of the Three Crowns. Then she smiled. "These are the real thing, all right. The kings must have visited Barry and given him the goggles. You were telling the truth."

"And I have a Spirit Flyer too," Barry said eagerly. He was glad to see that someone was beginning to believe him. John still frowned. "But he was trying to spy on us just yesterday," John objected. "And he acted like a traitor to Josh and Randy. How could he just switch like that?"

"Well, how does anyone change?" Susan responded. "I know that Josh and Randy were asking the kings to change Barry's heart. Remember? We were out at the farm all together a few days ago. You even joined in with them."

"Yeah, but did you think the kings would really do it?" John asked. "I mean, we know Barry better than Josh and Randy do, even if he is part of their family. We're the ones who've had to live around him all these years."

"Well, the kings can visit anyone," Susan said. "We just didn't believe it. Maybe we gave up too soon on Barry. At least Josh and Randy didn't give up asking."

"I don't know . . ." John said reluctantly. He stared at Barry with new interest. Susan smiled.

"You can wear these like regular goggles," Susan said to Barry. "Only you sometimes can see deeper. Go ahead and try."

"I didn't see anything different this time," Amy said, taking off the goggles. She had been listening to their conversation. "I still don't understand why they work sometimes and not other times."

"Barry should still try," Susan said.

Barry pulled on the goggles carefully. At first everything just seemed darker, as if he were looking through sunglasses. Then for a few seconds, everything got blurry and then came back into focus. Only this time Barry was quite surprised at what he saw. He quickly jerked the goggles up on his forehead. He looked very concerned and even worried.

"They must have worked," Susan said with a slight smile. "What did you see, Barry?"

"I'm not sure," Barry said truthfully. "All kinds of stuff." Without another word, he pulled the goggles back down over his eyes, and this time he left them there. He stared straight at the courthouse and then at the sky above it. Barry didn't know how to explain it, but he saw a gigantic black shadowy snake coming right out of the courthouse roof, as if the snake were a kind of ghost. Yet the darkness of the snake could be seen in every window of the building. The rest of the snake shot high up into the sky like a curling tower of darkness and shadow that disappeared into the gray clouds. As Barry looked at the sky, he saw other snakelike creatures of various sizes hovering there.

Barry watched the people going into the courthouse with their number cards. He saw great dark chains on their necks going all the way down to their feet. All these chains seemed to be connected to each other, pulling the people along in the line. The most frightening sight, however, was seeing all the shadowy black snakes resting on different people, adults and children alike. Some snakes were large and some small, some were wrapped around people's hands, while others were wrapped around their legs or neck or waist. Some of the strange ghost-snakes had bitten down into a person's body and hung on that way, as if they were leeches, sucking out the person's essence. The whole town square seemed to be filled with darkness and little wisps of smoky clouds, some of which twisted and turned like miniature tornadoes.

Then he saw a glare of bright light cutting into the darkness. Off to one side of the square he saw them coming. Barry stared in surprise. There were several men dressed in brilliant white clothes, and some were holding bright shining swords. These were just like the men that had helped Barry the day before. They looked strong and dangerous, like soldiers. They walked right into the square by the old wooden gazebo. And as they entered the square, all the dark shadowy snakes resting on people began to open their mouths and hiss at the approaching men of light. Barry realized that the snakes and the men of light were enemies. Coming behind the strange men in white clothes were several townspeople walking into the square.

"There's Daddy!" Susan Kramar said suddenly. Barry pulled up the goggles to look with his own eyes. Susan pointed to the southeast corner of the square near the gazebo. Barry looked where she was pointing. A large group of adults were walking into the square. They were walking in the same place the mysterious men of light had been, as if following them. Without the goggles, Barry didn't see the men with the swords, though he sensed they were still there. The front of the line stopped by the old wooden gazebo. There seemed to be at least a hundred or more townspeople coming down the street. Mr. Kramar was at the front. Barry wanted to use the goggles again, but he also wanted to see what was going on with his own eyes. Looking through the goggles was interesting, but also confusing and scary. He put them in his pocket and looked back at the adults marching into the square. He was surprised that some of the adults were riding Spirit Flyer bicycles. One of the men pulled a trash can closer to the sidewalk. Then he held up something in his hand for the others to see.

"That's Mr. Jones and he's holding a number card," John Kramar said. "But what's he doing with it?"

They all watched in surprise as the man threw the number card into the trash can. People all over the square were looking at Mr. Jones. The men in the gray ORDER uniforms looked especially interested. Mr. Jones turned and looked at the other men and women with him. Then they rushed forward, throwing their number cards in the trash can. Mr. Kramar threw in his card and stood beside Mr. Jones as the others came up to the can.

Suddenly, the level of noise rose in the square. Many of the people who had been standing in the line that led into the courthouse had gotten out of line to watch the others throwing away their number cards. Everyone was talking and pointing. The men in the gray ORDER uniforms began to look very nervous. Some were talking into walkie-talkies. Others were talking among themselves. One man took his rifle from his shoulder.

Captain Sharp came out of the courthouse and walked quickly down the steps. He burst through the crowd of people. A deep scowl was on his face as he strode over to the line of people who were throwing away their number cards. The people stopped as he approached them.

"I don't like the look of this," Susan said. "I think we'd better get out of here."

"Are you kidding?" John Kramar asked. "Uncle Bill may need us. If I had a number card I'd go over there and join them right now and throw mine away right under Captain Sharp's big nose."

Captain Sharp was talking to the people by the trash can, but the children couldn't hear what was being said. He abruptly walked away and went back into the courthouse.

The men and women by the trash can began throwing away their number cards again. The people who had been in line at the courthouse were moving slowly closer to watch them. Suddenly, smoke came out of the trash can.

"Someone must have tossed a match in there," John said excitedly. Great streams of tarry black smoke drifted up out of the can. The fire burned brighter. More and more number cards were dumped in to feed the flames. For an instant, Barry thought he saw his dad in the crowd near the trash can, but then a man in a gray ORDER uniform blocked his view.

Suddenly, everything seemed to happen at once. The sirens from the volunteer fire department began to blow and wail. As they did, the men in gray ORDER uniforms rushed toward the crowd of people who were burning their number cards. There were shouts and screams. Big military trucks roared into the square. More men in gray uniforms hopped out. There were so many people, Barry couldn't see what was going on.

"We'd better get out of here," Susan Kramar said loudly.

The children backed against the wall of the building. Barry tried to see what was happening. Everyone was heading toward the corner of the square where the smoke was floating up into the air. That's when Barry saw Sloan Favor and some other children on the other side of the square take rocks out of their brown paper bags. Barry was shocked when he saw Sloan toss the rock right through the big plate glass window of Mr. Jones' shop. Then more rocks were thrown. Screams filled the air as more military trucks came into the square. The men in gray uniforms poured out of the trucks, holding long black billy clubs. The whole square had become a place of confusion and panic. People were yelling and running in every direction.

Barry was even more surprised when a group of men in ORDER uniforms started running right at him and the other children. They didn't look very friendly.

"They threw rocks!" one of the men in the ORDER uniform shouted to the others, pointing at the kids on Spirit Flyer bikes.

"Run!" Susan screamed. In an instant, the kids on Spirit Flyer bikes were pedaling down the sidewalk. Barry was right in the middle of the pack. The whole group turned down the alley and began to pick up speed. The men in uniforms ran into the alley after them. Barry ran faster, though he knew he couldn't outrun a full-grown man for very long. Several of the Spirit Flyer bikes began to rise up into the air. Barry's heart pounded with fear.

"Get on," Susan yelled, slowing down next to Barry. Barry didn't hesitate. He swung his leg over and held on. Susan stood up on the pedals and the bike quickly picked up speed. The old balloon tires rose off the ground about six inches and the bike shot forward. Barry never looked back.

The group of riders split off into different directions as they came out of the alley at the other end. Susan followed John Kramar down Ninth Street.

"Can you take me home?" Barry asked. Susan nodded and turned the bike down the next street. In no time, they were on Barry's street. She glided up to his driveway and came to a stop. Barry hopped off.

"Thanks a lot," Barry said. "And thanks for believing me. I think I better just stay inside and wait for my parents to come home."

"That sounds like a good idea to me," Susan said. "I'll see you later." Susan turned her old Spirit Flyer bike around and headed back down the street.

Barry ran up the sidewalk, unlocked the door and let himself into the house. He went out to the garage. His Spirit Flyer bicycle was there. Barry then went into the kitchen to wait for his parents to come home.

He waited and waited and waited. He thought he heard the sound of a gun shot coming from outside. He checked all the doors several times to make sure that they were locked. Barry called Napoleon to sit with him on the couch. He scratched the dog's ears. An hour passed, then two hours. Barry tried calling the school, but got no answer. He heard a noise outside in the street. Barry looked out the front window. A large bus was parked in front of his house and a gray Security Squad truck was parked behind the bus.

Several men in gray ORDER uniforms walked briskly up to the front door. They knocked three times. Barry wasn't sure whether to answer or not. The knocking was louder the second time. Barry opened the door. He was surprised to see that Sloan Favor was standing next to the men.

"That's him," Sloan Favor said. "I saw him there this morning. He was one of those Spirit Flyer kids throwing rocks."

For a moment Barry was speechless. Then he felt indignant. "I didn't throw anything," Barry said.

"Barry Smedlowe, you'll have to come with us because you contributed to a disturbance in the town square this morning," a man in a

uniform said. "You can answer your charges at the ORDER Security Squad Center. Take him. We also have search warrants for this house to search for government papers and documents."

"Come with us," the Security Squad man said grimly. Sloan Favor smiled with satisfaction as Barry walked outside. They led Barry to the long gray bus and made him sit in the front seat. The bus was filled with children and some adults. Most of them Barry recognized as kids that had Spirit Flyer bicycles. They all stared at Barry silently. Some of them were crying or had been crying. At the back of the bus he saw John and Susan Kramar, Daniel Bayley and Amy Burke. Susan waved to Barry.

The bus pulled away from the curb. Barry saw four Security Squad men enter his house. Sloan Favor stood in his yard, still smiling. He waved his fist at the bus as it moved down the street.

A few minutes later the bus turned onto Cemetery Road. It passed the big Goliath factory and the Centerville Cemetery. Finally it slowed down as it reached the gray cement-block wall of the ORDER Security Squad Center. The gates to the compound opened slowly and the bus rolled inside. It stopped by the front doors of the large gray building.

The bus doors opened. The driver stood up. "Everyone out for processing," the driver said. "Let's go. Don't be wasting time."

Barry was the first one off the bus.

PRISON
SONG

• • • • • • • • •

19

Barry and the other people on the bus were herded into a large open room inside the gray Security Squad Center. The room was about the size of a gymnasium. The floor was bare gray cement, and the walls were gray cement block, just like the rest of the building. Since the building was so new, many areas inside weren't finished. On one side of the room was a set of steps that led up to rows of bleacherlike seats. In the middle of the seats on the front row was a special boxed area that hung down slightly lower than the other seats. There were six chairs in this spot, plus a stand-up lectern with a microphone.

The Security Squad men kept urging the bus riders along. They separated the adults from the children which made several of the children cry. One woman cried out.

"Don't take my baby," she yelled. "Don't take my baby!"

A little girl about five years old was pulled from the woman's arms. Two men took the woman by her arms and led her out of the room. Barry was shocked at the sight.

There were already several other adults and children in the large room. The adults were at one end of the room while the children were being kept at the opposite end. The room was filled with tension.

"You children stay behind this blue line on the floor," a man in a Security Squad uniform said He pointed at the line on the floor with a billy club.

Barry saw John and Susan Kramar, Daniel Bayley and Amy Burke. He walked over to them in the crowd of children.

"They got you too," Susan said sympathetically. "I knew as soon as the bus turned onto your street that they would go to your house. They picked up Amy before she even got home."

"They got a lot of people in this town," Daniel Bayley said solemnly. "But what are they going to do with us all? There must be over two hundred people in here."

"How can they arrest us?" Barry asked. "They accused me of throwing rocks in the town square this morning. I never did that."

"They accused us of the same thing," John said bitterly. "They said we helped cause a riot. Under emergency martial law they can arrest you for all kinds of reasons."

"My dad was one of the first ones to be arrested," Susan said. She was on the verge of crying. "I thought they were going to take my mom, but she's about to have a baby. Luckily Grandfather and Grandma Kramar are visiting and can help out. Lois and Katherine hid in the garage or they might have taken them too."

"They said they were going to search our house," Barry said. "I hope they don't steal stuff."

"Who knows what these goons will do?" Amy Burke said. "According to what I read in the paper, under these new emergency laws, they can keep you up to thirty days if they suspect you of committing some kind of crime."

"But we were just watching in the square," John Kramar said. "No one in our group threw rocks."

"Someone did," Susan said. "I couldn't believe the way the square looked when the bus drove through it. Lots of windows were broken and stuff inside the stores looked a mess. I heard some people say there was looting."

"I saw Sloan Favor and some of the other kids throw rocks in the windows," Barry said.

"Really?" Daniel asked. "When did you see it?"

"Right after that fire started in the trash can by the gazebo," Barry said. "When they rode into the square, a lot of the kids in the Super Wings Patrol were carrying paper bags. They were in line to register at the courthouse, but when things started to get wild I saw Sloan and some of his pals throw rocks and break a window."

"But they're blaming it on us," John said. "That's not fair."

Just then a group of men in gray uniforms entered the little set of box seats. Captain Sharp was with the group and stepped up to the microphone.

"Peace and safety," Captain Sharp said, crossing his arms over his chest. Someone in the crowd of adults booed loudly. Captain Sharp frowned as he looked over in that direction but then looked down at his clipboard. He began reading. "I am here to inform you that emergency martial law is and has been in effect in this county. All of you are charged with participating in unlawful assembly and conspiracy against government officials and conspiracy to disrupt legal governmental activities. Some of you will be charged with an even more serious offense of inciting a riot. You will be held here overnight as your papers are processed and then be taken to the state capitol where you will be held no longer than thirty days while you await a judgment from a court of emergency-law judges."

"Dictator!" someone shouted from the group of adults. "What about a fair trial?"

Captain Sharp frowned again, looking down on the crowd of Centerville citizens.

"None of you would be here if you were cooperative citizens and hadn't broken the law," Captain Sharp said coldly. "All of you had a chance to play by the rules, yet you chose to break those rules. We in the Security Squad have acted on behalf of the majority of the citizens of Centerville who are law-abiding people. You will soon find out that the people of this town and this nation will no longer tolerate lawbreakers and hoodlums."

Captain Sharp looked out over the children and at the group of adults. There was silence in the room.

"Children will be sleeping and eating in rooms on the third floor until they depart tomorrow morning," Captain Sharp said. "Adult males will be on the second floor and adult females on the first floor in the rooms provided. Before you are assigned to your quarters, you will have ten minutes to meet with the rest of your family members in this room. No visitors from the outside will be allowed to visit here. They will be allowed to visit you at state center if they fill out the appropriate paperwork and are approved by the governing board. Peace and safety."

Captain Sharp crossed his arms over his chest and walked briskly away from the microphone and out of the room.

The next ten minutes were quite confusing as parents and children were reunited. Barry wandered among the groups of families, looking frantically around the room. Finally he saw his father and mother and ran over to them.

Mrs. Smedlowe had been crying. She hugged Barry tightly. Mr. Smedlowe looked grim and unhappy.

"What's going to happen to us?" Barry asked. "Are we really going to get in trouble?"

"This whole thing is outrageous," Mr. Smedlowe said. His eyes were filled with a kind of fury Barry had never seen before in his dad. "They're treating us like common criminals, like common criminals. I never thought it would come to this."

"Josh warned us," Mrs. Smedlowe said, her voice cracking. "You read those documents."

"They accused me and a bunch of other kids of throwing rocks at the town square this morning," Barry said. "They came to the house and got me. But I didn't throw rocks. They said they were going to search the house. They showed me some papers."

"Well, they won't find what they're looking for," Mr. Smedlowe said with grim satisfaction.

"I want you to be brave, Barry," Mrs. Smedlowe said. She wiped her eyes with her handkerchief. "Everything will be all right. These people have made a big mistake, that's all."

A whistle blew. A man in a gray ORDER uniform stepped up to a microphone.

"All children, ages seventeen and under, are to exit at the east door, which is painted blue. All women will exit out the yellow door on the west. All men will wait until the others have gone."

Mrs. Smedlowe hugged Barry tightly. She didn't act like she was going to let go. "Everything will be all right," she said. Barry had never heard his mother talking in that tone of voice. "Just do what they tell you and don't cause any trouble. I love you, honey." Barry nodded. He suddenly felt very afraid and didn't want to leave his parents.

A Security Squad officer moving through the crowd stopped by them. "All children through that blue door," he said. Mrs. Smedlowe let Barry go.

"I'll see you later," Barry said, though in his heart he wasn't sure. He turned and joined the line of children going through the blue doorway.

After walking up several flights of steps, Barry and the other children entered a long narrow room with several short, little cotlike beds. There was a row of windows on one side of the cement-block walls. The windows were covered with heavy wire-mesh screens that looked like pieces of chain-link fence.

Two Security Squad men stood by the door. When all the children had come into the room, they shut the door.

"Find yourself a bed which you can use for the night," the man said loudly. "You will be having supper at five-thirty."

Barry sat down on a bed. The mattress seemed very hard and the pillow was very small. All the beds were the same. Barry put his jacket on the bed to claim it. Then he walked over to join the group of children by the window. John Kramar and some other boys were pointing toward the town. Barry looked silently at the water tower in the darkening sky. All the children were quiet.

At five-thirty they herded the children to a cafeteria. The children had thirty minutes to eat. The supper wasn't too bad, Barry thought. They had small hamburgers and cole slaw and peaches on a metal tray. The food reminded him of the food at the school cafeteria.

By the time they got back to their room, it was dark outside. There were no curtains and the windows showed the dark night. Barry sat down on his spare little bed and felt a wave of sadness and fear falling over him, just like the night. The other children seemed restless and afraid, and were unusually quiet.

A few rows over, Susan Kramar began singing a song. She sang softly at first. Barry had heard them singing that song before, about freedom and the kings and the gift of joy they had given to people. Some other children started to join in the song. Just listening to their sweet voices made Barry feel better. More and more children gathered around and began to sing.

Soon over half the room was singing about the glory and the wonders of the kings and all that they had done. Barry began to sing too. The song was easy. And the more he sang, the better he felt.

When it was over, Susan started another song and then another. The whole place was filled with their music. Children began to smile and hold hands. Barry smiled too. Somehow the night didn't seem as dark when they were singing. Barry was glad to say thank you to the Prince of Kings in a song.

Some children began to call out to the kings for freedom. Daniel Bayley asked out loud that the kings would knock down the walls of the Security Squad Center and free them. Other children repeated the same words. Even Barry called out finally.

"Free us from this prison," Barry said loudly. He was surprised how easy it was to say it.

Other children kept singing as if to drive back the darkness of the night. And as they sang, Barry touched his pocket. He still had the Spirit Flyer Vision goggles. He took them out and quickly slipped them on.

"They're here!" Barry said in surprise. He looked around the room again and again, hardly believing his eyes. Stationed all around the room were the men in white clothes who were smiling as they watched the children singing. They seemed very interested and were listening carefully. Many were by the windows, holding sharp shining swords.

"They're here," Barry said again, more excited. "They're all over the room."

"Who is here?" Susan Kramar asked when she saw Barry with the goggles. For a moment, everyone stopped singing.

"The men in white clothes," Barry said. "Look!"

He handed the goggles to Susan. She put them on and looked around the room. Then she smiled. A tear rolled down beneath the goggles on her cheek.

"It's the Aggeloi!" Susan said happily. Other children crowded around Susan.

"Let me see, let me see!" they said.

"May the others use your goggles?" Susan ask Barry. He nodded.

Susan began to sing again, louder than ever as she handed the goggles to a little boy. He looked through them and then let someone else look. All the children became more and more excited as they saw they weren't alone.

Soon everyone was singing loudly. A guard opened the door and started to quiet them, but for some reason, he didn't say anything and closed the door. But by then, Barry had the goggles again. He had seen the man in white clothes reach out and touch the guard's mouth.

Barry smiled. He sang loudly even though he wasn't really a very good singer. He didn't care. Then he saw someone else standing in the midst of all the singing children. The Prince of Kings stood there with a smile. Suddenly, all the children realized he was there. Barry took off his goggles but he could still see the Kingson who smiled at the children and stretched out his hand.

The whole room was suddenly quiet and waiting. Barry knelt down by his little bed and stared at the Kingson. Just looking brought a peace into the boy's heart that he didn't think was possible. At that moment, he realized that everything would be all right. No matter what happened to them, as long as the Prince of Kings was near, Barry knew that he could face any fear.

"Your deliverance is near," the Kingson said softly, but with a voice that no one would doubt. Everyone in the room heard it. The Kingson smiled again.

The children began to sing softly. They went to their beds quietly and lay down. The lights in the room went out but not the light in their hearts. Many were still singing even as they fell into a deep peaceful sleep.

MR. PEEK
AND MR. PENN
· · · · · · · ·
20

The long gray ORDER buses were parked and rumbling inside the Security Squad Center. Barry looked down at the buses from the window. On the front of each bus was the sign of the circled X, right below the windshield. He counted at least thirteen buses. Heavy woven wire that looked like chain-link fence covered every window of each bus except for the windshields.

Many of the other kids looked out the window at the buses. They had all heard that they were going to be shipped out that morning, right after they had eaten breakfast. Captain Sharp had said they would be going to the state capital and that judges there would decide their fate. Barry wished he could see his parents and find out what was going on.

John Kramar and Daniel Bayley and some other children were sitting together. They had been talking, but they began to sing. Barry went over to listen. He didn't know the song, but it was a pretty melody. Barry just sat and listened, wondering about Josh and Randy. Christmas was just a few days away, and it seemed so wrong that they should be locked up. Hearing the song made him feel better. He remembered what the Kingson had said the night before.

John and the other kids didn't say anything but launched into another song. By the time they were almost finished with the third song, Arthur Masters, a third grader sitting by the window, jumped up.

"There are people out in the road," Arthur shouted. Everyone stopped singing and rushed over to the window. Barry was amazed. It seemed like more than half of the town of Centerville was gathering outside the gates. More were arriving in cars and trucks and many on foot.

"My grandfather's out there!" John Kramar said excitedly. "He's on that red tractor in front of the gate. They must not have arrested him."

Barry looked closer. He recognized the old man sitting on the tractor. And down below on the ground, he was sure he saw Mr. Peek and Mr. Penn, the attorneys his father knew. Barry was sure it was them because they both wore red suspenders. He was surprised that they were both sitting on old red Spirit Flyer bicycles.

"I wonder what's going on?" Susan Kramar asked.

"It looks like the whole town is coming out to see what's happening," Daniel Bayley said.

Several men in gray ORDER uniforms moved closer to the gate. They were all holding weapons. Captain Sharp walked quickly across the gravel parking lot. He stopped at the gate and began talking. After a few minutes, he opened the gate a crack and two men followed him inside.

"That's Mr. Peek and Mr. Penn, Attorneys-at-Law," Barry said. "They tried to help get Josh and Randy free earlier this week."

"Maybe they will get us out," Susan said. "The Kingson said he would deliver us."

The children stayed glued to the window. More and more people came down Cemetery Road from town. They all stood outside the gray cement-block walls and seemed to be waiting. Anxious soldiers gathered inside the walls, close to the gate.

Captain Sharp went back outside. He spoke to the men in uniforms, and they quickly turned and walked away from the gate.

Just then, the big metal doors opened behind the children. A man in a gray ORDER uniform gave the ORDER salute.

"Peace and safety," he announced. "You are all to get whatever things you have and follow me. You're going home."

"All right!" John Kramar said with a smile. Everyone ran for the door. Barry was near the end of the line. The children walked down a hall and down some steps. They walked down another hall and into the big main room that seemed like a gymnasium. The adults were already waiting. Barry saw his parents and ran to them. They all hugged each other fiercely for a long moment.

"Are you all right, son?" Mr. Smedlowe asked.

"Yes," Barry said. "We slept in these little hard beds. The Aggeloi stayed with us and the Prince of Kings himself came and visited us. He told us we would be freed. And he must have meant soon. Are we really going home?"

"Yes," Mr. Smedlowe said. "Finally these men are coming to their senses."

Captain Sharp came into the room and walked up the steps and over to the speaker's platform. He crossed his chest with his arms. "Peace and safety," he said quickly. No one returned the greeting. The crowd was silent, waiting. The Captain cleared his throat. "The government has decided to release you all today rather than process your cases at the capital," Captain Sharp said, reading from a piece of paper on a clipboard. "You will all be on suspended probation. Since this is a first offense for most of you, and this is considered a holiday season for some, the state has decided to be lenient on your behalf. But you are hereby warned that these acts have gone on your records. It is well within our legal rights under emergency law to keep you and press charges against all of you. If further infractions of the law occur in the future, your negative record of points from this incident will count against you. So I advise you to be on good behavior and cooperate with the government and with progress. Let's all be good citizens and try our best to make this a better world. You are free to go. Peace and safety to you all."

The Captain crossed his chest once more and walked quickly down the steps and out of the room. Everyone talked at once as they headed toward the doors. Barry jumped up, trying to see through the crowd.

"I don't see Josh and Randy," Barry said.

"You mean they weren't with you and the other children?" Mrs. Smedlowe asked.

Barry shook his head. John Kramar walked by and Barry grabbed his arm. "I don't see Josh and Randy," Barry said. "Have you seen them?"

John shook his head. Susan hadn't seen them either. Mr. Kramar shook hands with Mr. Smedlowe.

"Good news after all," Mr. Kramar said.

"It is for us," Mr. Smedlowe replied. "But we haven't been able to locate our nephews, Josh and Randy."

Most of the people had filed outside by then, all except the Smedlowes and the Kramars. Mr. Peek and Mr. Penn were standing just inside the front door. Mr. Peek had his thumbs tucked behind his red suspenders and was calling out names of people as they passed by. Mr. Penn checked off the names of the people on a long list.

"The Smedlowes and the Kramars," Mr. Peek said with a smile.

"Check and check," Mr. Penn said. He put his ink pen back in his pocket. "That's everyone."

"What about Josh and Randy?" Barry asked.

Mr. Peek pulled on his short gray beard. "We weren't able to get them released," Mr. Peek said slowly. "We concentrated just on those who were taken in yesterday."

"I won't go unless Josh and Randy can come too," Barry said suddenly. "It's not fair. They belong with us."

Captain Sharp walked down a hall just then, accompanied by an old gray-headed man that Barry knew was Mr. Cyrus Cutright, the president of the Goliath factory. Captain Sharp stared at the Smedlowes and the Kramars and then turned to Mr. Peek and Mr. Penn.

"Everything in order?" Captain Sharp asked tersely. His face was unhappy.

"Where are Josh and Randy?" Barry demanded. He knew he was interrupting, but he didn't care.

"The case of your cousins is still being processed," Captain Sharp said.

"You've had them long enough," Barry said. "I'm not leaving unless you let them come with us. In fact, you can keep me with them. Or better yet, let them go and let me stay here in their place."

Everyone was surprised by Barry's sudden outburst. John Kramar looked at him with surprise.

"So you want to stay, do you, boy?" Captain Sharp asked. For a moment, he looked so angry, his eyes seemed to glow red. Barry blinked in surprise.

"Barry, you don't mean that," Mrs. Smedlowe said.

"Yes, I do," Barry said. "Why couldn't I stay? At least until after Christmas. They've been in here long enough. They shouldn't have to miss Christmas because of me. It's all my fault that they're here in the first place."

"We did have another motion we were planning to file later today on Josh and Randy's behalf," Mr. Peek said to Captain Sharp. "Even under emergency law we've found a provision for cases such as this."

No one said anything for a moment. Outside the gate, the crowd of people was still waiting. Captain Sharp looked over at the crowd and frowned. Cyrus Cutright was watching the crowd of people by the gate also. The old man looked at Barry with contempt.

"You lawyer fellas come inside and show me what you got," Mr. Cutright said in his raspy voice. "You come along too, Mr. Smedlowe."

The men went back inside the building. Captain Sharp looked at Barry with disgust and followed the other men inside, closing the door behind him.

Barry held his mother's hand and squeezed it. Mrs. Smedlowe squeezed back. John and Susan Kramar walked over to Barry as they waited.

"I guess I was kind of hard on you the other day," John Kramar said to Barry. "I'm sorry I didn't believe you had a Spirit Flyer and all."

"I don't blame you," Barry said. "I would have done the same thing if I was you." John reached out to shake hands. Barry smiled. The two boys shook hands. Then Barry shook hands with Susan.

"You have to come to our next meeting," Susan said excitedly. "It's kind of like a club."

Susan began telling him about their Spirit Flyer meetings. But then the door opened. Josh and Randy walked outside, their faces lit up in big grins. Mr. Smedlowe was also grinning.

Barry immediately went over to Josh and Randy and stood before them. He tried to speak, but found that he had a lump in his throat. Tears filled his eyes. Josh looked at his cousin in surprise.

"I'm sorry. I—" Barry choked and couldn't finish. He looked down.

"It's ok, Buurrry," Randy said, moving to Barry's side. The little boy hugged Barry around the waist. "We love Buurrry."

"Sure we do," Josh said. He reached over and patted Barry on the back. Together the three boys walked toward the gate. The Smedlowes and the Kramars followed. As they walked outside, the waiting crowd began to cheer. Grandfather Kramar honked the horn on the old red tractor. Barry and the others laughed at the odd but joyful sound.

Mr. Peek and Mr. Penn stood by the front door of the Security Squad Center. They signed some papers and gave them to Captain Sharp. The

Captain grunted but did not speak. Mr. Peek and Mr. Penn, Attorneys-at-Law, walked slowly toward the gate.

"I believe I'm ready for an early lunch," Mr. Peek said, pulling back on his red suspenders.

"I'm not surprised," responded Mr. Penn. "We've already done a good day's work, I believe. And it's my turn to buy. After you, Mr. Peek."

The two lawyers walked through the gate. The crowd roared and cheered and clapped as the two attorneys joined them. Several people rushed up to offer their thanks and congratulations.

Back inside the Security Squad Center, Captain Sharp stood by the door and watched the townspeople heading back toward their homes. Mr. Cyrus Cutright stood beside him. The old man lit up a cigar and began to smoke.

"I still say we should have shipped the whole bunch out," Captain Sharp said bitterly.

"Orders are orders," Mr. Cutright said sourly. "I don't know why the Bureau changed its mind. It makes us look like a bunch of fools, if you ask me. But I think we got a clear message across, anyway. They said they were already crowded down at the camps down by the capital. And with all those townspeople watching, we didn't want to risk some other kind of disturbance, or we'll be the ones that are shipped out of here. Maybe we were moving too fast."

"My boys could have taken care of any trouble," Captain Sharp said. "I think we should have dealt with it now. Next time they may be stronger."

"They'll all come on line, sooner or later," the old man said. "Once we shift over entirely to the New Point System, they'll have to play by our rules. Time is on our side. A few country simpletons can't stop progress. Besides, it will go over well if they think we let them go as some Christmas holiday favor."

"Christmas!" Captain Sharp snorted with disgust. "This will be the last Christmas those traitors will ever see. Mark my words. They got off easy this time, but next time they'll be mine. You just wait."

Cyrus Cutright nodded. The old man tapped some ashes into his hand, then held the hand up to his open mouth and tossed the contents into his mouth. He chewed the ashes with a bitter smile and swallowed.

Captain Sharp made his hands into fists. He watched in silent fury while the people headed to their homes. Soon Cemetery Road was empty under the clear December sky.

CHRISTMAS GIFTS
• • • • • • • •

21

A few days later, Christmas arrived. Several families were invited out to the Kramar farm outside of town. Barry and his parents and Josh and Randy all went to a party at the old workshop. The Smedlowes drove, but Barry and his cousins insisted on riding their Spirit Flyers. Mr. Smedlowe was skeptical about the boys' tales of the wonderful powers of the bicycles, yet he finally agreed, even though snow had begun falling that morning.

Barry, Josh and Randy rode down the driveway together. Barry thought they would head out to Crofts Road and then fly to the farm. But as they rolled into the street, Barry's bicycle suddenly took off, as if it had a mind of its own. "Hey, this bike is going by itself," Barry said with concern. He pushed back on the brake, and although the bike slowed down, it didn't stop.

"Let it take you where it wants," Josh said as he pedaled alongside his cousin. "Sometimes Spirit Flyers do that. You'll be all right."

"Are you sure?" Barry asked nervously. Though he had ridden his Spirit Flyer a lot in the last few days, he was still discovering how it worked. He got a better grip on the mysterious old bicycle.

"Sure, I'm sure," Josh said with a smile.

The red Spirit Flyer carried Barry over to Main Street and then turned toward the town square. Barry held on tightly as the bike moved toward the center of town. Josh and Randy easily kept up. Barry was surprised when the old red bicycle turned down Ninth Street and into the alley behind the toy store.

"Oh, no," Barry said softly as he saw several shiny bicycles parked by the old wooden shack that had once been his clubhouse. Even Josh looked worried as the bike carried Barry down the alley. Sloan and the other kids were outside and saw Barry coming. Sloan quickly bent down and picked up a rock. Barry and the bicycle stopped a few feet away from the leader of the Super Wings Patrol. Josh and Randy pulled up behind Barry.

"What do you Rank Blank jailbirds want?" Sloan snarled. Sloan lifted his arm as if he would throw the rock. He seemed surprised when Barry didn't react. Barry had always been a cowardly bully as far as Sloan was concerned.

Barry wasn't sure what he was supposed to do or why the bicycle had brought him to the alley. He was surprised that when he saw Sloan and the other boys, he wasn't afraid like he would have been in the past. The old wooden shack looked pathetic and dingy.

"You want to try and steal my clubhouse again?" Sloan asked.

"No," Barry said simply. "It's yours. It's what you deserve."

"What do you mean by that?" Sloan asked suspiciously.

Barry smiled. He suddenly began to realize why the old red bicycle had brought him back to the alley, to the place of his defeat. Sloan and the other boys stared at Barry.

"It's all yours," Barry said happily. "Merry Christmas! Merry Christmas to you all."

Without another word, Barry turned and began to pedal away. Sloan threw the rock. It thudded into Barry's back. The rock stung. Barry stopped and looked back at Sloan and his old friends. They were bracing themselves for a fight. Some of them looked embarrassed because of Sloan's cowardly attack. But Barry didn't feel the anger he expected. He stared at the other boys until many of them looked away.

"See you guys later," Barry said. He turned around and began pedaling again. Sloan picked up another rock, but as he looked at the questioning faces of the kids in his patrol, he dropped the rock.

Barry was smiling as they rode out of the alley. The three boys rode out of town down Crofts Road toward the Sleepy Eye River. Before they got to the bridge, they pointed the handlebars upward and the bikes rose quietly into the falling flakes of snow. Barry pedaled faster and the bike shot up twenty feet over the bridge and river. Josh and Randy were right behind him. By the time they reached the row of trees beyond the river, the three boys were a hundred feet in the air and still going higher and faster.

They reached the Kramar farm sooner than Barry expected. The speed and wonderful nature of the old red bike still delighted and amazed the boy. He didn't want to land so soon. He circled around in the falling snow, filled with a deep joy. The other kids down below saw the Smedlowes flying high above and got on their bikes to join them. Soon the air was filled with the old red bicycles and the shouts of children, excited about Christmas. They immediately began playing a game of flight tag. The falling snow didn't slow anyone down. When Grandfather Kramar arrived, he gave the younger children rides on his old red Spirit Flyer Harvester.

Later on, it was time to eat. The families gathered around the long table. Everyone feasted on hot turkey, ham, delicious vegetables and bread. When they were all done eating, Grandfather Kramar stood up at the end of the table.

"We have a lot to celebrate," Grandfather Kramar said with an easy smile. "Not only is this the day we celebrate a very special birthday of long ago, but it's also the birthday today of a new Kramar. Little Paul Nathaniel Kramar was born early this Christmas morning to Bill and Betty Kramar. She'd be here, but she's resting in the house."

Everyone clapped for a long time. Some people whistled.

"Many of you can also celebrate your release from the Security Squad Center," the old man said. Everyone was quiet. Some people nodded their heads. Many of the children smiled. "That was a gift of the kings to this whole town. And now I think the kings have something else to show us."

Grandfather Kramar walked across the side of the room where his old red tractor, the Spirit Flyer Harvester, was parked. Everyone gathered around. He got up on the seat and looked out at the room full of people.

"No matter what happens in the days ahead, the kings have been reminding me of something they've shown me, and I think they want to show us all," Grandfather Kramar said. "I think Christmas is one of the best days to see it."

The old man bowed his head silently. Barry, like everyone else, waited. Then Grandfather Kramar turned on the light switch of the old tractor. There was a hum, and Barry thought he felt something like wind sweep through the room. But he didn't see anything. He expected to see the lights of the big old tractor come on. But there didn't seem to be anything happening.

"Watch for the small signs," Grandfather Kramar said. "Watch for the small signs in the heavens."

Everyone waited. Instead of the room getting brighter, it got darker and darker. In the darkness, tiny lights appeared above their heads. The lights looked vaguely familiar. Then Barry recognized them.

"It's the sky at nighttime," Barry whispered. "Those are stars, aren't they?"

The sight reminded Barry of the planetarium at the state capital he had visited on a school field trip in fifth grade.

"Watch for the small signs," Grandfather Kramar said softly.

Barry looked up at the stars. Then he noticed that one star was moving. The single star kept getting brighter and brighter as it seemed to get closer. Everyone in the room was staring at it. As the light got brighter, something seemed to change in the room. Everyone was totally quiet as they watched the approaching star in the midst of the other twinkling stars.

The star came closer and closer and soon filled a third of the night sky. Barry realized it wasn't just an ordinary star or comet. As the star came closer, it was filled with a royal presence, the Prince of Kings himself. He was coming toward them in a blaze of glory. Barry stared with deep awe into the light and saw him. But this time the Prince was different. He was shining with brightness and power, clothed in brilliant shining white clothes. His eyes blazed with fire, and he held stars in his right hand. Then he spoke with a voice sounding older than time.

"Fear not," the Kingson said, the words sounding like the waters of a crashing waterfall. "The first time I came in secret and weakness. But the second time I come in power and might, as King, to plunder evil and injustice, as one who reclaims his throne. The time is set and was set from the beginning when I threw out the fireball from my hand. In a twinkling all the heavens and earth will melt. In a twinkling I will come and set up my throne."

Barry could no longer look because the light grew so bright and the presence of the Kingson was so awesome and mighty. The boy felt himself sinking down toward the floor as the Kingson came closer.

He wasn't sure how much time had passed, but Barry sat up and looked around. For a moment he wasn't sure where he was. Then he remembered. All over the room, people were sitting on the floor. Some still seemed to be asleep, as if they had fainted. Grandfather Kramar sat in the seat of the old red tractor. He smiled at Barry and winked.

One by one, people got up. No one spoke. There was a great silence in the room that was the silence of respect and fear and awe.

"The kings have blessed us with a mighty vision of what's to come," Grandfather Kramar said. "He told us not to fear because he's returning to set up his throne. I think hearing about his return will be a great gift and blessing for us all in the days to come. So let's not forget his coming."

"Who could forget a sight like that?" John Kramar murmured to Barry. "I thought this whole room was going to burn to a crisp or explode or something. Didn't you feel it?"

All the other children nodded and began whispering. Everyone agreed they had never seen such a sight.

"And that was just like a preview," Daniel Bayley said with a soft voice. "Just think of what it will be like when it's really time."

The room was silent once more as people thought about the small star that announced the return of the king. Barry didn't think he could ever forget the powerful way the Kingson had looked.

"That was a Christmas gift from the kings to us all," Grandfather Kramar said. "I understand there are more gifts to be opened. I think it's time."

There was a pile of presents around a Christmas tree at the end of the workshop. Everyone gathered around. Different presents were passed out. And as people opened their gifts, they shared what that day meant to them.

Josh and Randy both received new coats and warm leather gloves. Randy looked especially pleased as he tried on the gloves. The little boy was already dreaming of the snowballs he would throw. Josh looked around the room and smiled.

"To me, the gift I'm really enjoying today is having so many new friends," Josh said.

"Me too," Randy agreed. The little boy looked up at his brother, then squeezed Barry's hand. Barry squeezed his hand back.

When it was Barry's turn, he knew what he wanted to say. He cleared his throat. He was surprised that he wasn't afraid to speak in front of so many people. Even though he barely knew many of them in the room, he knew that they accepted him.

"I'm thankful for my Spirit Flyer, of course, even if it is a kind of strange old bicycle," Barry said. A lot of people smiled. "But I think the best gift to me is forgiveness for the things I did to hurt other people and the kings. When Kingson gave me those gold coins, I knew he paid for all the pain I had caused others. I didn't know that such forgiveness was really possible. And since he freed me from the chain, I haven't felt as afraid as I used to feel. Now I feel free. I never knew the chain made me such a slave to my fears. But since he broke it, I really feel different."

The other children nodded and smiled.

"The love of the kings casts out all fear," Susan said with a smile. "Their love is our gift too."

Barry smiled. Josh and Randy leaned over and hugged him. Barry knew he was enjoying the most precious of all gifts, the love of the kings.

Once the gifts had been opened, everyone got cups of hot cider and went outside, gathering around a large bonfire. While the delicate snowflakes fell, they began to sing. They sang songs of thanks and songs about the Kingson. They celebrated his first coming and they celebrated his return. They knew that no matter what troubles happened in the world, they were citizens of the kingdom which stretched beyond the world and beyond time.

The bonfire blazed up into the winter night. Barry sang the loudest of all that Christmas eve because he felt like he had the most reasons of all to be thankful. He sang without fear or shame because he knew the price had been paid. For the first time that he could remember, he knew he was free, free in the love that casts out all fear.